18158

F   Haycraft, Molly
HAY   Costain

      The King's daughters

DATE			
MAR 21 '75			
DEC 2 '77			
OCT 5 '79			
OCT 26 '79			
OCT 5 '84			
NOV 22 '85			
DEC 6 '85			
OCT 8 '91			

The King's Daughters

By Molly Costain Haycraft

The King's Daughters

Molly
Costain
Haycraft

J. B. LIPPINCOTT COMPANY
Philadelphia and New York

For Jay

The King's Daughters

One

My sister Eleanora raised her face for her lord's kiss, and I, standing nearby, felt my eleven-year-old heart swell with joy at the sight of its radiance. The pealing of the bells, as we then left the church, seemed to be telling all Bristol—indeed, all England—that King Edward I's oldest daughter was now married to the Duke of Bar, the man she loved, and I remember almost skipping down the long aisle and into the September sunshine where our chariots awaited us.

The glow still pervaded me when I followed my other three sisters into the retiring room at the castle to freshen up before the lengthy banquet, and I smiled delightedly at them.

"Have you ever seen Eleanora look more beautiful—or more happy?"

"As indeed she should, Bette. She's unbelievably lucky and she knows it!" Joanna replied bitterly. "First to have Alphonso of Aragon die after so many years of betrothal; then to be allowed to make a marriage of affection. Our parents were not that generous to *me!* Oh, no! They tied me to Gilbert de Clare the moment they heard of Hartman's death in Germany, and I need not tell you, I'm sure, what a cat-and-dog life we lead together."

"But you do l-lead it here at home," interrupted Meg, the stammer she had inherited from our father a little in evidence. He had trained her, as he had trained himself, to control it by his choice of words, but when she spoke impulsively it was still there. "Your lot as the Countess of Gloucester is b-better than mine, I assure you, for I l-loathe my lord, too, and one of these days Jean and I must g-go to Brabant and probably never s-see England again!"

Mary, who had been adjusting her rich nun's habit before a polished silver mirror, turned to them and gave a grim little laugh. "If you'd been forced to take the veil when you were only seven you might well complain. Think of *my* way of life before you talk of hating your husbands. Never to hold a child of my own in my arms—"

Her voice broke, and as I listened to all of them and looked from one discontented face to another—Joanna's so strikingly handsome with the black eyes, lashes, and brows; Mary, plump but comely under her nun's headdress; and Meg, dear Meg, the plainest of the family, marred by the twisted lip handed along to her by our lady mother—my feeling of elation ebbed away.

Until that moment I had not thought very much what

it meant to be a king's daughter, although I, myself, had been betrothed to Jan, the heir of the Earl of Holland, since my third birthday. I had always known, to be sure, that like Meg I must someday wed him and leave England, but that someday was off in the dim future, so far off that something might happen. Not that I hoped Jan would die; he was a stupid boy, yes, a silly boy, but not even I could wish that.

Then, however, hearing Joanna and Margaret discussing their unhappy marriages, I think I saw, for the first time, that mine could be equally unhappy; and when we took our seats on the dais I caught myself staring at Lord Gilbert and Lord Jean, their two husbands, and comparing them with my young betrothed.

The Earl of Gloucester was, of course, a much older man; he had been wed and divorced long before he and Joanna were married and could almost have been her father. All the de Clares were redheaded; Gilbert was actually called "Gilbert the Red," and his long, horselike face had a weathered appearance, lined and splotched with rusty freckles. According to Joanna he had the usual hot temper that goes with red hair, and as she certainly has one, too, passed on to her by the Spanish side of our family, I could imagine that their life together was one series of verbal battles.

My eyes passed lightly over Duke Jean's ugly fat face, for I had never enjoyed looking at *him*. He had visited my brother and me often enough at Langley—our favorite residence—for me to know that Meg was right when she said he was both cruel and self-indulgent.

Because Edward and I are the last two children in a very large family, our parents having had twelve in all, although only five girls and one boy lived beyond early childhood, he and I shared a household of our own. It has been customary for the heir to the throne to live in a separate establishment, but as Eleanora, Joanna, Margaret, and Mary were no longer in the nursery when I and then he was born, it seemed sensible to bring us up together.

This does not mean that he and I were strangers to our family. Indeed, in our early years hardly a month passed without either a visit from our parents or one or all of our sisters or a visit of ours to wherever our father was holding Court. Not that visiting or being visited is the same as living under one roof; I never shared my sisters' chambers, beds, or confidences.

I am aware now that Joanna disliked Earl Gilbert long before they were wed and that Meg hated Jean from the time soon after their first meeting when she overheard him jeering at her stammer and slightly twisted lip. Why my sister should inherit both these family defects and the rest of us escape them altogether I do not know! It still angers me and always will.

Although Edward was only six and I only eight in the year 1290, we were present both at Clerkenwell when Joanna became the Countess of Gloucester, in what was almost a private ceremony, and, a few months later, at Westminster Abbey to watch Meg marry Jean of Brabant.

I find I recall little of Jo's simple wedding, but Meg's I shall never forget, for it was held with the greatest pomp and followed by the most lavish celebration London had ever witnessed. My brother and I rode into town attended by eighty knights, every other high-ranking noble brought many more, and I have since heard that at least seven hundred knights and ladies as well as a thousand wealthy townspeople took part in the day's festivities.

Of all the marching through the streets, solemn vows, singing, dancing, and eating, however, the memorable moment for little Edward and me was when Master John Brodeye, our best pastry chef, carried into the banquet hall an elaborate model of one of our castles, complete with towers, turrets, flying pennants on the battlements, moat, drawbridge, and all, made out of spun sugar and marzipan.

As he set it proudly before his Queen, she burst into instant admiration.

"Magnificent! Truly magnificent! The finest subtlety I have ever seen!"

Then, while Master Brodeye retired, smiling gratefully, she beamed down the table at us.

"Thank you, my dear children. It is too beautiful to eat."

I can still see her loving face. Some months later, when she fell ill of a virulent fever near the town of Grantham and died there, I cried bitterly because I was not at her bedside to bid her farewell. Now, recalling that moment we shared at Meg's wedding feast, I am glad that I carry *it* in my heart and not a picture of her wasted face, stilled by death.

But, oh, how I mourned! How everyone mourned! Of my father's overwhelming grief I need say nothing: the proof of it stands at each place where his "chere reine" rested on her last, lengthy journey from Grantham to Westminster—thirteen crosses erected to her memory.

I am sure, that night, he missed her even more deeply

than usual, realizing how she would have rejoiced at the knowledge that one of her daughters was marrying a man she loved. It would, I think, have eased some of the pain of seeing what I saw: Jo and Meg sitting with forced smiles on their faces, their eyes bleak, beside the husbands they loathed.

What, I wondered, would she have thought of my chances of being content in the marriage she and my sire arranged for me so long ago? As I asked myself that question I turned to Jan, who was so intent on his food that he remained unaware of my scrutiny. That he was handsome I had to admit: tall, for eleven, thin, his hair as fair as mine, his eyes as blue.

But when he glanced up from his silver platter there was the usual vacant expression in those blue eyes, and his mouth, as he stopped chewing, fell open and remained that way. I suppressed a sigh of distaste and, being only eleven, decided to allow the future to take care of itself; this was Eleanora's wonderful wedding feast, and I should now enjoy every minute left of it!

− In the months that followed my oldest sister's marriage I succeeded very well in putting the dread of my own out of my mind. The Lord Henry returned to Bar in November to prepare for his bride's arrival there, and it was not until the middle of April that we finally said farewell to Eleanora. She, of course, was so eager to be with her new husband that there were few tears shed at her departure, and although Meg smiled grimly when Eleanora told us she looked forward to the day when we should all meet at

Brabant, Holland, or Bar, I was able to kiss her warmly and echo her words.

After that I threw myself into my old comfortable way of life with my brother Edward, our most serious problem being whether we should hawk or play games by the fire. The summer came and went; autumn passed; it was winter again. Still the months flew by unheeded, and I was, I think, in my fourteenth year before the clouds began to gather over my head, ending my carefree childhood.

What so disturbed my peace of mind was a conversation between Meg and our father, a conversation at which I was present—and which I shall never forget. My sister, strangely enough, was still in England, and so was her husband, even though it was now five years since their marriage and more than a year since the death of Jean's father during a tournament honoring Eleanora's arrival in her new home had made Jean Brabant's Duke.

Meg had come to us at Langley, as she often did, and without her husband, which was also usually the case. Not long after her arrival, however, a messenger came bringing word of the imminent appearance there of Duke Jean, and my sister, looking exasperated, announced that she would depart immediately.

"Return with me to Westminster," she suggested. "Let Edward entertain Jean. The less I see of my lord the happier I am!"

Not being eager to welcome Duke Jean myself, I accepted Meg's invitation and we were on our way within the hour. It was one of those rare beautiful days in late February when everything smells of the coming spring, and although the roads were still at their winter worst, the sun lifted our spirits and turned the journey into a pleasure jaunt. And as Langley was only a little more than twelve miles from Westminster, an easy distance in good weather, we arrived at the palace by midafternoon.

Having left most of my attendants behind me—Meg's retinue was more than sufficient for us both—I was housed, for the first time, in Maiden Hall, the apartments set aside for the King's oldest unmarried daughter. They were small but charmingly furnished, situated in a remote, secluded wing of that rambling old palace beside the Thames. They had been Eleanora's until her household became too numerous, and I had always envied her their comfort; our mother had covered the stone walls with tapestries to keep out some of the damp and had placed among our plainer English things a few of the low, heavily carved tables that she brought home from Acre after the Crusade. Her orders to keep fires burning there until midsummer were still obeyed, five years after her death, and I entered to find it delightfully warm.

Learning that our father was in Essex, we ordered a simple supper and ate it by ourselves at my fireside, chatting contentedly over delicious cold chicken and jelly. Even before we were finished I was yawning openly and was just about to suggest retiring early when one of our ushers entered and informed us that the King had returned to the palace.

"His Grace awaits you in the Painted Chamber," he said. "Follow me, my ladies, if you please."

The Painted Chamber was our father's beautiful bedchamber, the pride and joy of our grandfather, King Henry III, so elaborately decorated that I found something fresh to admire every time I entered it. There were angels on the ceiling, the four Evangelists on the walls, Edward the Confessor's coronation over the royal bed, two lifelike

lions facing each other in a gable, and tonight I saw some
Bible texts on the window jambs. The whole room was a
blaze of scarlet, mazarine blue, gold, and silver.

"I did not expect to find you here, my daughters," said
our sire, after kissing us. As he straightened up, I marveled
again at how tall and handsome he still was, and how abun-
dant his hair, although it was now quite dark. I remembered
it when it was golden yellow and when he seemed to me a
giant! Well, he had always towered head and shoulders over
most men and was often called "Longshanks" for his unusually long legs. While I was thinking this, he spoke to Meg.

"Why this sudden change of plans, Margaret? Assuming
you would be at Langley for at least a se'nnight, I sent Duke
Jean to you there with a most important message from
me."

Moving her gray eyes away from his, Meg replied a little
hesitantly. "I did intend to remain there, dear Sire, b-but
—" Then, as if making a decision, she raised her head and
continued, almost defiantly, "If you m-must know, I came
away to avoid Jean! Surely I need not t-tell you that we
are happier apart? Everyone knows that b-by now!"

Our father sighed heavily and dropped into a chair. "Sit
down—and you, too, Bette." For a moment he just sat
there, drumming his long fingers on the table in front of
him. Instead of anger there was sadness in his face; his left
eyelid, which always drooped a bit, as did his father's before him, now half covered his eye.

"Yes, daughter," he replied finally, "I do know that you
and Jean are happier apart. Neither of you has made any
secret of that fact in the years since you were wed, and
that is one reason why I have allowed you both to take
your time about settling down together, hoping that if I
showed you understanding and tolerance you might show

it to each other and ease the problems between you, whatever they are. The people of Brabant have long been urging me to send them their Duke and Duchess—and have shown increasing impatience at Jean's reluctance to go home. As indeed they should! Jean is now twenty-five years of age; you are twenty; it is more than a year since his father's death. He is their ruler and should be in Brabant, not England."

"Then send him!" said Meg abruptly.

"I shall. He goes, in fact, in a few weeks, and you go with him. That, my dear child, is what he went to Langley today to tell you. Three of our largest and most seaworthy ships are being readied to take you and your possessions and your people. I was off inspecting them myself."

I was watching my sister as our father talked. All the color drained out of her cheeks, and her gray eyes, her only claim to beauty, turned almost black. For a minute or two she stared at him in silence; then, with a despairing sob, she buried her face in her hands and began to weep so violently that her sandy braids fell forward over her bent shoulders.

My father rose and went to her. "Now, Meg, now, child! Surely you knew this day must come?" Leaning over her, he patted her heaving back awkwardly, his countenance both disturbed and impatient. "Eleanora is not far from Brabant, Bette will soon be marrying Jan and on her way to Holland, and I may well have business there myself before long. It is not the end of the world."

Meg raised tear-drenched eyes and shook her head.

"You don't understand—you just don't understand! If I go to Brabant I must l-live with Jean, live with him all the time. And I *hate* him, Sire, I truly hate him! If you must know, we despise each other and have from the f-first day we met as children!" She was speaking so fiercely that, when she continued, her stammer grew much worse. "He l-laughed at my s-s-stammer and called me c-crooked lip in front of everyone!"

"As you say yourself, Meg, you were children. All children are cruel to each other." He shrugged his wide shoulders. "It means nothing."

"It means my flesh crawls when he touches m-me! Which, thank God, is not often. He's too busy tumbling every kitchen wench he can l-lay his fat hands on, and annoying my ladies and m-maids."

'A wife shuts her eyes to such matters. Surely your mother, God rest her soul, told you—" He began to pace up and down the room. "You are the King's daughter, my child I love you and I want you to be happy, but I dare not put your happiness before the good of our country. If we are to be at peace with our neighbors, trade with them, see England secure and prosperous, it is my duty, among other things, to arrange alliances that will make us all one family. You cannot think that I want to s-send you away!"

As he broke off suddenly, the "s" sound and his emotions betrayed him and he, too, stammered slightly. Meg rose, threw herself into his arms, and sobbed on his shoulder.

"Then let me remain a little longer—just a l-little longer, if you love me! S-send Jean to Brabant and give me a few peaceful months with you before I g-go."

He held her close, dropped a kiss on top of her head, then freed himself. "A few months then, Meg. But you must promise to spare me these scenes. When I next say you must go, you go!"

$\mathcal{T}_{wo}$

$\mathcal{M}$eg's husband sailed for Brabant a few weeks later, and although I shared in my sister's relief I found my own peace of mind shaken. Even before we left our father that evening I began to think of *my* future, realizing that I would soon be facing what Meg faced and fearing that I would be equally unhappy. After listening to his words, particularly when he said, "Bette will soon be on her way to Holland," I knew I could no longer tell myself that my marriage was something to worry about in the dim years ahead—that it might never happen—that my betrothed, like Alphonso of Aragon and Hartman of Germany could well die before the knot was tied.

I had, after all, good reason to know that this was most

unlikely; I saw Jan often enough to be aware that he was in the best of health—that although he was, certainly, a fool and a weakling, unable to make up his mind about anything, he had an extremely strong body.

Unlike Meg's Jean, whose face was so fat that his little black eyes looked like currants stuck in dough, and whose dark over-curly hair was parted most unbecomingly in the center of his round head, making him look even uglier than need be, my Jan was not unpleasing in his visage or person. His features were almost handsome, although his blue eyes had such a vacant expression; his chin receded slightly, and he had never outgrown a childlike way of allowing his mouth to hang open.

I did not hate him, but I neither liked nor respected him. When we met at Court as small children we were both too shy to say anything much to each other, and later, when we were paired to dance during the Christmas revels, he usually interspersed his few remarks with an awkward laugh that I found quite irritating. No doubt there were things about me that he disliked, but he did not let me know what they were.

Until that first night at Maiden Hall I had shut my eyes to the fact that I was old enough, at thirteen, for marriage. Now I knew that Meg was right in saying so, and I lay awake until dawn brooding about it, turning cold at the thought of sharing a bed with Jan.

I think I left my childhood behind me that night; certainly I rose the next morning and discovered that I was looking at everyone and everything with different eyes. My life was the same; the change was in me.

Edward seemed younger, suddenly, too young to talk

to. Our games lost their interest for me and I felt awkward with the other lads in our household, having to make an actual effort to behave as usual with them.

Fortunately Meg was with us most of that spring and summer. This made it easier for me, as did several weeks we all spent together in the Tower of London, an interruption in our usual life that I heartily welcomed.

Later, after we returned to Langley, our sister Mary and three of her nuns paid us a lengthy visit; then, just before they left us to ride back to Amesbury, our father arrived unexpectedly.

"It is good to find four of my children under one roof," he said to us, "and to know that my other two daughters are happily occupied with *their* children."

This was true of Eleanora, who now had two infants, but Meg told Mary and me afterwards that Earl Gilbert and Jo were quarreling even more than usual.

✳

The rest of that year of 1295 was uneventful; then, at its close, we learned that Jo's stormy marriage was over. Her husband died at Monmouth Castle after a brief illness and, after burying him at Tewksbury with the other de Clares, she came to our father's Court.

Her visit was a short one, its purpose to make sure that she received her great inheritance from her late lord. Once that was arranged she returned to Monmouth immediately, and, despite our father's wish that she now reside at Bristol Castle to enable him to keep in touch with her and his three grandchildren, she insisted on remaining there, writing him one excuse after another.

Then, in March, the Scots began to ravage Cumberland

and attack Carlisle, and faced with this more serious problem our sire, I suspect, forgot Joanna's willful disobedience

Hearing that the Scots were also making secret advances to France, my father marched north without delay, wasting no time in nipping the whole insurrection in the bud He took Berwick first; then, after an eight-day seige, Edinburgh Castle fell into his hands; and on the tenth day of July the whole of Scotland formally surrendered to him at Montrose

Taking their Stone of Scone away with him as a symbol of his supremacy, our father the King marched around the rebellious countryside, setting up a fresh government for its people before coming home. This accomplished, he returned to London and, soon after his arrival there, summoned Edward and me to the Tower to join his Court.

As we were at Mortlake at the time, my brother turned to me and smiled. "We'll go by water," he said. "Thank God we have some settled weather at last."

It had been an unusually wet summer, but this particular August day was clear and almost hot, so warm, in fact, that I remained under the striped canvas awning shading the deck of our gaily painted barge most of the way along the Thames.

After we passed Westminster, our palace there looking quiet and deserted, I followed Edward to the prow and stood beside him for the remainder of the short journey, shutting my eyes as we came in sight of the dried-up heads stuck in a row on London Bridge, then clinging to him for support while we made our way under its arches, our oarsmen fighting the treacherous current that always threatened to hurl our barge against the slimy stonework.

Safely back in quieter water, we waved and bowed to a

cheering crowd of townspeople already lining the banks from the Bridge to the Tower, having heard, I suppose, that England's heir was on his way by river. This particular stretch of the Thames was filled with wherries, loaded barges, lighters, tilt boats, and—as it was not yet sunset, when they must tie up for the night—the small craft of the watermen, seeking passengers from water stairs to water stairs.

It was too busy here for the families of swans we had passed earlier, sailing serenely along with their curved necks held high, but we saw and heard even more gulls, screaming like hungry infants as they circled and swooped overhead.

Actually, I felt relieved the moment we slipped through the water gate at the Tower and left the din behind. Our ears, however, were again assaulted as we entered the huge stone keep and began to follow our usher up the one narrow staircase that served the whole building. This was because the royal family was only a minor part of its occupants: there were prisoners in the small, chill, damp chambers that filled the floor at water level; England's money was minted here; the Crown jewels were housed and guarded; the Admiralty, the War Office, and many more of our officials carried on their share of our country's affairs under its roof.

To us, trying to make our way up to our apartments situated above the banqueting hall, council chamber, lesser hall of the justiciars, and the smaller rooms that accommodated their serving people and clerks, the business of the Tower seemed to mean a constant climbing up and down the stairs by everyone concerned.

However, we eventually mounted the final step, passed

St. John's Chapel, and hurried along the dim, narrow passage to our familiar and sadly uncomfortable chambers, thanking God that it was August and not January. There was a huge fireplace in the banqueting hall, the only one in the whole Tower, but what warmth it threw out was confined to the hall itself, and even there one was apt to shiver and shake during the colder months.

We had learned, as children, to wear our warmest woolen gowns at the Tower—and often our cloaks! And I still remember my Spanish-born mother bewailing the chill river breezes that, no matter how many tapestries she hung on the stone walls, somehow reached us wherever we sat, turning our feet and hands to ice, making it impossible to do our needlework or even practice on our lutes.

Today it was merely dank, so, with only a passing regret for the drier, prettier rooms of Maiden Hall at Westminster, I chatted idly with Meg, who joined us there, and with my ladies, while my tiring women unpacked the gown I would wear to supper.

My father never dressed as befitted his high station and in his plain, short-sleeved tunics—often drab in color— could have been taken for a simple townsman; but despite this he neither expected nor desired his ladies to follow his example and was always pleased to see us in rich fabrics and soft furs, adorned with the beautiful jewels he himself bestowed on us.

Once, when I was a small child, I asked him why he never wore his crown or the ermine-banded velvet robes I saw on many of our nobles. He smiled and replied, "I should not be a better man, my daughter, however splendidly I was dressed."

I can still hear his words and see his dark eyes, soft and

full of love as they met mine, his handsome nose, large but well-shaped, and his firm chin, all but hidden in a short trimmed beard. And I know now what I was too young to realize then, that England never had a better king or a better man, that no daughter ever had a better father, and no wife a better husband. It has been said that he equaled Henry II as an administrator and had the personal prowess of King Richard, the great Lion Heart.

Then I think how Joanna, Meg, and I often behaved, marveling at his patience and remembering how seldom he lost his temper with us.

He was to lose it later that evening at the Tower, although there was certainly no hint of any trouble during supper. After welcoming us warmly he seated Edward beside him and Meg and me nearby, talked some of his recent campaign in Scotland, then listened, with a rather drawn face, I thought, to a song or two by our musicians.

Rising early, he dismissed the company and bade Edward good night. "Come with me to my privy chamber, Bette— and you, too, Meg," he said, turning to us. "We have all had a wearying day, I know, so I will not keep you from your beds any longer than need be."

As we followed him from the hall I glanced at Meg, raising my eyebrows in question. She merely shrugged her shoulders and shook her head. Whatever our father had on his mind was apparently not known to her, and so we walked along behind him in uneasy silence.

I suppose I expected his chamber to be empty. I have not forgotten how my heart sank when we entered it and I saw Jan, my young betrothed, Earl John of Holland, awaiting us there. He had not been at supper—in fact, the last I had heard he was at Windsor hunting with his gentlemen, and we had not met for some months.

While he kissed my hand I tried to greet him in a seemly manner, but, as always, the words came stiffly to my reluctant lips and I fear my smile was a feeble one. A moment later I noticed that there was no smile of any kind on his face, and it seemed to me that there was a suggestion of redness about his eyes. He had always been one to show his shallow feelings readily, but I asked myself whether any lad of nearly fifteen, even Jan, would actually weep.

Moving to his side, my father patted him on the shoulder. "Early yesterday Jan and I received some very sad—some very shocking and tragic news from Holland. Earl Florence, God rest his soul, has been most cruelly and foully slain, why or by whom we have not yet ascertained, and your lord, Elizabeth, is now Holland's ruler."

Aware, even in this first moment of horror, of what I must do, I knelt before Jan and murmured a few phrases of sorrow at his bereavement. That he had loved his father dearly I knew, and I was truly sorry for him. He raised me immediately, muttering something in reply, and Meg, in her turn, said all that was proper.

When we had finished our little speeches of sympathy, our father patted Jan again and suggested that he retire. "We need not intrude on your grief any longer, my son," he said kindly. "You and I will have much to decide soon, but these are early days still."

He waited until my young lord had bowed his way out and the sound of his footsteps had died away before speaking again. "Well, my dear daughters," he said at last, his voice heavy, "this grim event in Holland means, I am afraid, that I shall lose you both in the near future. My friends there are already urging Jan's return, and when he goes he must take his wife with him."

I raised my head to protest, but he silenced me with a wave of his hand.

"You and Earl John are old enough to wed, Elizabeth, and there is every reason for the marriage to take place as soon as possible. He will go home prepared to remain there —and with his Countess at his side."

He paused for a moment, then turned to Meg.

"And you, Margaret, must take this opportunity to make your long-delayed journey to Brabant. When Jan and Bette sail, you shall sail with them."

"But—my lord—!" Meg's voice broke a little and her eyes pleaded with him. "You p-promised I might wait and accompany *you!*"

"At that time I expected to set out for Flanders this summer. As indeed I would have, had not the Scots kept me busy in the north."

"Then let me remain until—"

"No, Margaret, no!" My father's face darkened angrily as he fairly shouted his refusal. "I have given in to you about this much too often. You have had your way over and over again, and now I will not listen to another word on the subject. Not one more word, Meg. When I say you go, *you go!*"

Three

*M*y only comfort during the long wakeful hours that followed my father's preemptory announcement was the hope that something might still happen to delay my marriage. And even *that* faint comfort soon began to dwindle away, for we were almost immediately caught up in the always lengthy and elaborate preparations for a royal wedding—my wedding, alas—and both the time and place for it were settled.

"Parliament meets at St. Edmundsbury in November," my father said one morning to Meg and me, "so I have invited the leading nobles and burgesses from Holland and Zealand to join me there, as we must consult on their country's problems and on the details of Bette's nuptials. Your ships, my dear child, will sail from Harwich, the best port by far for Holland, and for this reason, and because I will already be in that vicinity, we have decided that Ipswich is the most convenient city for the ceremony."

"In November?" asked Meg in despairing tones.

"No, no," was our father's immediate response. "Not that soon, Meg. I'll hold my Christmas Court at Ipswich first, and we'll celebrate the New Year there together. Then, if the date suits Jan's friends, he and Bette will be married on the eighth day of January. Joanna must come to us, of course, and Mary, if she can be spared."

It was now October, and, before any of us had written to Joanna to inform her of my father's plans, one of her squires arrived at Court with a letter from her. His name was Ralph de Monthermer, and she had sent him down from Monmouth to be knighted. Whatever were her reasons, and my father did not discuss the matter with us, they were apparently good enough to convince him that the young man deserved the honor, and, after complying with our sister's request, he presented the new Sir Ralph de Monthermer to us.

He was, I remember thinking at the time, a very pleasant and handsome man, with such an air of self-assurance and dignity that I could well believe him worthy of his title. We chatted with him for only a moment or two, however, and, when he had promised to carry letters and messages back to Monmouth for us, we thanked him and bade him farewell, saying to each other afterwards that Joanna was fortunate in having him in her household

The next few weeks were such busy ones that I had little opportunity to brood. Meg was with me, too, which made it more convenient for the tradesmen who were providing us with our fresh wardrobes, jewels, chariots, furniture for our chapels and kitchens—all the hundreds of items we would take with us to our new homes—and certainly made us both somewhat happier.

I still ache when I think of the hours we spent on our feet being fitted by tailors and seamstresses; and I shall never forget the sick feeling that swept over me every time I was asked to choose from the rolls of cloth of gold, silver, tulle silk, heavy silk, velvet, and soft woolens of all colors, woven especially for my long underrobes, surtunics, and mantles. Even the touch of the gleaming brown marten pelts and snowy ermine began to depress me, for I knew that I would be wearing the garments they adorned as Jan's wife, and in faraway Holland.

Our days, after a while, were not so wearying, and instead of falling asleep the moment I climbed into bed I found myself lying wide awake for what seemed like hours, making myself miserable by picturing my life with poor, stupid Jan. I wept and tossed, tossed and wept, and Meg, seeing my red, swollen eyes morning after morning, merely shook her head a bit grimly, her own eyes only too understanding.

I had long since stopped asking her about marriage. Her answers to my questions were so frightening that I was more than content to avoid the subject and relieved when she said nothing about my obvious unhappiness.

Inevitably the time arrived when we must set out for Ipswich. Many of our nobles, having returned home after Parliament was dissolved, were now on their way back there, accompanied by their wives and entourages of varying sizes, to share in the holiday festivities and attend my wedding. They were coming from all over England, of course, but the greater number would be traveling on the London road, making progress on it slow and difficult.

To ensure a swifter and more comfortable journey for us, therefore, it had been decided that Meg and I and our households (and our vast belongings) should sail as far as Harwich on the ships that were to take us to Holland later.

This was a fleet of considerable size: besides the *Swan of Yarmouth*, a vessel so large that it required a crew of fifty-three trained seamen, we had been provided with six other big ships, several barges, and numerous smaller craft. Much of the food for the sea voyage was, we were told, already on board: thirty-nine oxen, fifty-seven sheep, and more eggs, fowl, and fish than I could enumerate. Provender for our horses, firewood, and other provisions would, I learned, be taken on at Harwich during the weeks the ships would lie there at anchor.

Because our *Swan of Yarmouth* was heavily loaded and because we hugged the coast all the way, our short water journey was smooth and uneventful. The December skies were gray and chill, of course, but despite that and my dread of the near future I found my spirits rising. Two of our maids—one in Meg's retinue and one in mine—were to be wed at Court, too, and to accompany us, with their new husbands, to Holland and Brabant. They, Lady Eleanore de Burgh and Margaret Sackville, were fortunate girls as they were well content with the men chosen for them by their parents, and their gay chatter and happy faces rapidly dispelled my gloom. In fact I began to wonder whether I should not try to forget Meg's wretched experience. After all, our parents had learned to love each other very deeply. If we tried, even Jan and I might grow fonder.

By the time we disembarked at Harwich and were helped into the rowing boats that were to take us up the river to Ipswich, I was more cheerful than I had been since the day I learned my wedding date had been settled. It is difficult for a fifteen-year-old maiden to feel dismal in a group of holiday makers, and when the others began to sing in unison to the chant of the oarsmen I joined in almost wholeheartedly.

The skies were darker now, and before long light flakes of snow powdered our fur mantles and clung briefly to our eyelashes. It was cold in our open boats, very, very cold, but despite this we continued to sing and laugh all the way to our destination, where I returned my father's welcoming kiss with a warm one of my own and showed him a smiling face.

"It is good to see you looking well and happy," he told me in his most approving voice, kissing me again.

"I'm not *happy*, my lord," I replied, "but I'm determined not to spoil these last weeks with you. I want to enjoy every possible minute."

"And so you shall, Bette. We must make this a Christmas to remember always!"

It was apparent that everyone concerned felt the same way. The castle was already in its Christmas dress, its halls lavishly decorated with our scarlet-berried holly, trailing ivy, and every other kind of green branches that were to be found in the nearby forests; and fresh rushes mixed with fragrant herbs covered the cold stone floors. I remember strolling from chamber to chamber just for the delight of smelling the herbs I was crushing underfoot and the pungent scent of the newly cut pine lining the walls.

As I walked I heard our Joculator Regis, my lord father's chief juggler, alternately scolding and praising his animals and birds as he taught them new tricks for our entertainment, and, when he felt they were ready, doing much the same with his tumblers, glee women, and balancing girls. In another part of the castle our musicians practiced constantly, untiringly, and it seemed to me that even the servants performed their daily tasks with a cheerful willingness.

With each day bringing more guests, my casual strolls came to an end; every time I looked down into the great, crowded, noisy courtyard I saw another group of lords and ladies riding in under the raised portcullis, followed by their knights, squires, men-at-arms, servants, and baggage wagons, and before long it was impossible to make one's way through the corridors without the assistance of an usher.

The long tables in the dining hall were filled and more were set up; and although Meg and I, at first, sat one on each side of our father there came an evening when we had to surrender our places of honor to England's two most powerful noblemen: Roger le Bigod, Earl of Norfolk, England's Marshal, and Humphrey de Bohun, Earl of Hereford, its Constable.

My new seat was farther down the high table beside Lady Alice, the sharp-nosed shrewish Countess of Norfolk, known to all of us for her insatiable curiosity. I endured, as always, her prying questions, replying politely but telling her as little of my private affairs as I could. Then, swallowing a sigh of relief, I turned to my other table companion.

He was the Earl of Hereford's young son Humphrey, and, as his mother was a cousin of my late dear mother, a cousin of mine.

For a moment we smiled at each other; he studied my face, I his. I was the first to break the short silence.

"Have I changed as much as you have, my lord? I remember a small boy with knobby arms and legs and black hair that always needed combing." I did not add that I now found him very handsome indeed—but it was certainly true. In the years since we had last met, which probably was when I was eight or nine and he, I suppose, eleven or twelve, he had become a man. And, as I have just said, a *very* handsome man! The unruly hair was tamed, his bones well covered, and his visage unusually pleasing. There was warm laughter in the deeply set gray eyes now meeting mine, his nose was straight, and his clean-shaven chin all that a man's chin should be, neither jutting nor receding.

"If I commented freely on your changes, Cousin," was his answer, "you would freeze me with an icy glance. And quite rightly so! But I will tell you what *I* remember: a fair-haired, blue-eyed, shrill-voiced child without any knobs any place, who thought she could ride and hawk better than any of us—"

"Because I could!" I interrupted promptly. "Have you forgotten the time you fell off your pony jumping that little trickle of a stream?"

"No, nor the way you laughed, small beast that you were! Young Edward, too—where is he tonight? I thought to find him here."

"On the road from Langley with Earl John and our guests from Holland. But what of your lady mother, Humphrey? Did she not accompany you?"

He shook his dark head. "It's a long, wearying journey from Hereford, and she has not been in the best of health recently. However, I bring you her love, Cousin Bette, and her hopes that you will be happy in your new life."

Flushing slightly, I dropped my eyes. What could I say to this pleasant friend from my childhood? That I had no real hope of finding any happiness with Jan? The subject made me feel awkward, and, while I was trying to think of some way of changing it, he spoke again.

"I bring you something else—a gift from the Lady Joanna."

"Joanna? My sister?" I stared at him, surprised. "But why should you carry something for her when she will join us here very soon?"

It was his turn to look surprised. "Your father has not told you? Urgent business keeps her in Monmouth, I believe."

"Urgent business? Urgent enough to prevent her coming to my wedding? What could it possibly be?"

I saw him open his mouth as if to reply, then close it again, apparently deciding not to tell me whatever had been on his lips. I was about to press him further when a troupe of dancers entered the hall and made any more conversation difficult.

Later, however, I discussed the matter with Meg, who had already learned from our father that Joanna would not come to Ipswich. She shrugged away my suggestion that Humphrey de Bohun could tell us why, reminding me of our sister's behavior when she, Meg, had married.

"Earl Gilbert came in great s-state with six of their ladies and more than a hundred knights, but Joanna angered our p-parents by staying at home. They actually refused to send her the s-seven robes made for her for the festivities!"

I had forgotten completely. Perhaps, Meg and I now decided, Joanna had been so miserable with her husband that she was unwilling then and even now to watch us being caught in the same trap.

"She was well aware of my dislike for Jean," said Meg. "And she has encountered J-Jan often enough to know that your feeling for him can, at best, be only toleration."

Any doubts that I might have had of her love for me were dispelled the moment we unwrapped her gift. We both gasped.

"Curtains for your chariot, Bette—what s-silk, what embroidery! Joanna has made many beautiful things, but never anything as m-magnificent as this."

Our ladies clustered around us, adding their comments to Meg's.

"Thousands of stitches. It would take *me* a lifetime!"

"There's every flower here that I know, and every shade of every color!"

Each strip of heavy silk was, in truth, a flower garden, and I found myself wishing I had had a Spanish *gouvernante* like Joanna's Lady Edline to teach me how to create such beauty and how to find the enjoyment in it that was, we knew, Joanna's greatest pleasure.

"This," said Meg's Lady Eleanore, "must have been the Countess' chief occupation during her year of mourning. I suppose she needed something difficult to do at such a sad time."

When our father saw Joanna's enchanting gift he said very little, and it seemed to me there was a strained look around his eyes and mouth every time we mentioned her name. Meg noticed it, too, but she thought it had nothing to do with our sister.

"He has much to worry him," she told me. "Our clergy are refusing him the m-money he needs for his French expedition, and he has given them until sometime in January to change their m-minds. This whole year has been full of problems, and he continues to m-miss our mother."

Our brother and my future husband Jan arrived a few days before Christmas, making our company complete. I cannot begin to describe the confusion that now reigned at Ipswich Castle and in the town that lay just outside its walls, nor can I do justice to the lavish feasts spread before us each night or to the hours of delightful entertainment that followed them.

I know that I, sitting (as I must) beside my betrothed, was so enthralled by our Joculator's animals that I was able to laugh with Jan almost as if we were the happy couple we appeared to be. There was an amazing horse, I remember, that actually walked a tightrope, another that stood on its hind legs and played a tune on a small drum with its front feet, and a third that reared up and danced in time to our musicians' most stately measure.

We both chuckled over these antics while the hall was being cleared of the tables, and when my lord led me out to begin the Danse au Virlet I sang my verse merrily and gave him a warm smile as he finished his. When Jan sang, one forgot his foolish ways and weak face, for he had a truly beautiful voice; and he was, as well, such an unusually nimble dancer that I was almost sorry when we returned to our seats.

My happy mood enabled me to welcome each new partner with genuine enthusiasm—even my thirteen-year old brother! We, of course, were so accustomed to dancing together that our steps matched quite well, which was not the case with all the young noblemen who claimed my hand.

The clumsiest, I was surprised to discover, was Humphrey de Bohun. As the Master of the Dance led him to my side the musicians struck up the lively Danse au Chapelet, and before we had finished the first measure he had twice trodden on the tail of my gown. Instead of blushing over his awkwardness, however, he took it all in good part, and before long we were laughing together over his mistakes. During the slower measures I began to warn him of what he must do next, and this, as well, he accepted gratefully.

"Now you should kiss me," I murmured as the dance drew to an end.

"The one thing I need not be told!" he replied softly, his eyes alight with amusement. And while every other lord bent down and kissed his lady, my partner pressed his lips lightly to mine, as was the custom, then deeply—which certainly was not. Instead of moving away I allowed my lips to respond, answering his kiss with one of my own.

We both came to our senses almost instantly, but when we followed the rest of the company from the floor it was in a strained silence. The merry mood between us was gone. I, shaken still and more than a little ashamed, raised my eyes to Humphrey's only briefly as we parted; the laughter in his had disappeared completely, I saw, and was replaced by something quite, quite different.

Four

$\mathcal{H}$ad I been older—or wiser—I would have given little thought to Humphrey's disturbing kiss. As it was I let myself linger over it and relive it, experiencing again the warm response, the tantalizing and delightful feeling that I cannot describe. I was also young enough and foolish enough to look for him wherever I went, hoping I know not for what but unable to prevent myself from doing it.

Nor was I able to regain the pleasant ease with Jan that we had enjoyed together before my dance with Humphrey. The sight of his face, I must confess, annoyed me even more than ever now, and I was silently critical of every word he said.

I can only compare my state at this time to what it

would have been had I been suffering from a fever, and I remember Meg watching me, her own face anxious, as I wandered restlessly around the hall, glancing briefly at one group of lords and ladies, then another, looking, although I did not tell her so, for a glimpse of Humphrey.

He was usually there, of course, but he was never again seated near me at the high table, and although we danced together whenever the Master of the Dance partnered us —no one may *ask* the King's daughter to dance—we moved through the figures stiffly and almost silently. He seemed to avoid my eyes, and when he *did* speak it was only to make the usual comments on the music or the weather.

The weather, by the way, was all we could have asked; more light snow fell on the evening before Christmas, and we awakened the next morning to a crisp, clear, white world. At no time was the courtyard covered with more than a thin layer of snow, and this, naturally, soon disappeared, making it possible for everyone to move about freely. We could see from the castle lancets, however, that the surrounding countryside and the roofs of the houses in the town retained their snowy cover, which added vastly to our holiday mood.

The revelry, begun the night before, continued through the day: the huge steaming bowls of wassail were emptied and refilled constantly; the halls were crowded with our guests and innumerable townspeople, all, or so it sounded to me, shouting at the tops of their voices. The portcullis had been raised early, the drawbridge lowered, the gates opened; everyone from Norfolk and Suffolk was welcome to come and go at will, to mingle with their King's family and to share in my lord father's Christmas Court. This, I hasten to say, was as it should be, for they had agreed to bear most of the cost of my wedding celebration—a heavy, heavy burden!

I was standing with my brother Edward and two of his favorite companions, Perrot Gaveston and Aymar de Valence, when a very rowdy group of men and women entered the hall, their laughter and singing drowning out even the music of Edward's Genoese fiddlers, who were only a few yards away, playing especially for us.

It was Aymar, called by many "Joseph the Jew" because he had such a large hooked nose, who first noticed something strange about them. "Mother of God!" he said softly. "Am I seeing aright? The men are in women's garb, the women in men's."

Our startled eyes followed his. Mumming at holiday time was to be expected, but we had never before seen this done. A member of the Earl of Norfolk's household, joining us at that moment, was not surprised at all.

"It's a Christmas custom in these parts," he explained. "It began in the north—Scotland, I believe. Our townspeople exchange habits and go from house to house, partaking of holiday cheer. An innocent sport, although some of the older people frown on it."

After chatting a moment longer he strolled away and we stood in silence, still watching the same group. Perrot leaned over and whispered something in Edward's ear, which seemed to please and amuse my young brother, for he nodded and turned to me, his face alight.

"Find Meg," Edward told me briskly, "and those of your ladies who can hold their tongues and might enjoy an adventure. We'll slip into town later when the revels here are at their height. Why not? I'd like to try this form of mumming!"

I shook my head. "We'd be missed. Surely we'd be missed."

"Not tonight," interjected Aymar firmly, catching fire from my brother. "The Master of the Dance told me that the dining hall will be so crowded that our company will dance in all the adjacent chambers—even some of the corridors."

"I still don't think—" I began, protesting again.

"If you're too chickenhearted, Bette, remain here," interrupted Edward impatiently. "We can find plenty of other maids who will be more than willing to change gowns with us and venture into town. We'll keep our hoods close around our faces, and no one should be any the wiser."

My brother was, after all, too young to be considered guilty of anything by taking part in such an adventure except, perhaps, behavior ill fitting the King's son and heir For me it was another matter, but the prospect was too tempting to refuse. I would soon be far away, never to be young and gay and reckless again!

"Let me ask Meg," I replied weakly. "If she agrees, I shall, too."

To my surprise Meg not only agreed, she was delighted with the scheme, and a few hours later, having changed our clothing in remote apartments discovered by Perrot Gaveston, the men sending us their robes and cloaks, we sending them ours, we climbed down the winding stone staircase and, mingling with a stream of visitors leaving the castle, made our way through the gates and over the drawbridge without being questioned or even noticed.

There were a dozen of us: six lads and six maids, all in the highest of spirits. Who the other three young men were, I did not know, for the corridor at the top of the stairs where we gathered, after robing, was dimly lit by one flambeau. All I could see was a group of hooded figures ready to lead the way.

Now that we were outside the castle, we paused and allowed the strangers to move on ahead into the winding, busy streets which seemed to be as full of merrymakers as the huge building we had just left. While we stood, discussing in whispers what to do next, the door of a house nearby burst open and several people poured out, calling gay good nights to those inside.

As we watched and listened they made their noisy way to a second house and banged on its door until it swung wide to admit them, the sound of music and voices within making it obvious that others had preceded them there.

"Come!" I heard Aymar's voice say, and we surged after his tall cloaked shoulders, shouting and laughing ourselves as the townspeople had done, just reaching the still-open doorway before the last of the revelers disappeared inside.

A minute later we, too, were being warmly welcomed by a smiling host and his plump wife and urged into what seemed to be a sea of faces swimming in a great cloud of smoke. Every bench was full, as was the space around the fire, blazing so hotly in the center of the chamber that only part of the smoke found its way up to the low, raftered ceiling.

My eyes began to smart immediately. I glanced around for the others in our party and, finding Aymar de Valence at my elbow, asked him how long we must remain.

He indicated a table at the end of the small hall on which stood the usual bowl of wassail. "After we've shared a goblet with mine host I think we'll all be eager to move to a less crowded spot."

I nodded gratefully and moved closer to the door, hoping to find it less smoky there, then stepped slightly aside as it was flung open again to admit more guests. The new group of mummers was the one we had watched at the castle, and it was only too apparent to me that they had visited many other homes in the meantime.

Men and women alike were roaring drunk, and before I knew it I was trapped in the center of their rollicking company. A rough hand pushed back my hood, a red-bearded face bent down, breathing foul stale wine fumes into mine, and two bleary piglike eyes lit up in sudden triumph.

"A maid, a maid! And all mine—I saw her first, lads, I saw her first! Out mumming, my pretty? Just come with me, sweeting, and I'll show you some new tricks!"

I reached for my hood, trying at the same time to escape from his clasp and to find help, calling "Meg! Edward!" as loudly as I could in the overwhelming din. But I was encircled in a huge arm and swept through the partly open door almost as I opened my mouth to cry out.

Once outside I began to kick, struggle, and scream, hitting wildly at him with both hands. To my horror, I saw that the narrow street was now empty and the nearest houses dark. Laughing, my captor dragged me a few steps farther, catching both my hands in one of his hairy paws, and lowered his horrible wet mouth to mine while his other hand fumbled for my breast inside my cloak.

Shaken with fright and sick with disgust, I tried again to free myself—to evade that loathsome hand, to bite his lip, to dodge his hot animal kisses—

I think I was on the verge of fainting when I heard footsteps on the cobbles, a shout, and found myself as suddenly released as I had been captured. A tall hooded figure was

raining blows on the head and face of my would-be rav-
isher, who, apparently too startled and drunk to defend
himself, reeled around, tripped on the tail of the woman's
gown he was wearing, recovered his balance somehow, and
fled, running down the road away from the castle.

I cowered back into the shadows, wondering, as I tried
to regain my composure, what was facing me now. Had
this tall stranger rescued me for his own pleasure? Should
I run?

"I thank God, my lady," said a blessedly familiar voice,
"that I was watching you when that scurvy knave dragged
you from the house It happened so swiftly that I'm sure
only his drunken friends saw it. In any case, our companions were so hemmed in at the table that no one else
could have reached you in time."

"I am the one to thank God, my lord," I replied in
trembling tones. "I struggled, but he was too strong for
me. Oh, Humphrey, this was a mad thing for us to do! I
should not have come! I knew I should not have come!"

"No, perhaps not. But it seemed like an innocent adventure to me, and I thought with twelve of us together
we could come to no harm. Shall we go now and find the
Lady Margaret?"

"Don't ask me to enter that house again, please. I
couldn't! But I must not spoil your pleasure; if you would
just escort me back to the castle and then rejoin the
others—"

I was shivering so violently by this time that my teeth
chattered and my legs shook under me. Humphrey, with
a smothered exclamation, drew my cloak closer around
me, his touch so gentle that what little composure I had
regained deserted me and I burst into tears.

Without either of us seeming to move we were in each other's arms, I sobbing on his shoulder, he cradling me in a protective clasp and murmuring disjointed words of comfort into my ear.

After a moment I raised my head and tried to pull away. "I'm s-sorry, Humphrey, for being such a fool. But—"

Instead of replying or releasing me, his arms tightened and his lips found mine, and for the second time that night I was ruthlessly kissed. To my shame I responded instantly, melting closely into his embrace and answering his hungry kisses with fervent kisses of my own. I was still shaking when he paused, at last, but for an entirely different reason.

"Oh, Humphrey!" was all I could say. "Oh, Humphrey!"

He said nothing and I could feel him trembling, too, as we just stood there in the darkness, our arms around each other. Finally he gave a great sigh and moved away.

"I'm the one to be sorry, my lady. And I'm the fool." His voice was grim, almost bitter. "Forgive me if you can, and forget this ever happened. Come. Give me your hand, keep that hood over your face, and we'll slip into the castle while the gate is still open."

His words chilled me at first; then I began to realize with what rare understanding and forbearance he was behaving. I obeyed him at once, placing my fingers in his warm ones and hurrying along beside him over the rough cobbles.

"Our robes, Humphrey! What will my ladies say at the castle?" I slackened my pace, as this horrifying thought came to me, and tried to see his face in the dimness.

"We must find some place to change," he replied. "It—it just so happens that I am wearing yours. I chose them, wanting—"

Giving a rapturous gasp, I threw myself back into his arms.

"No," he said. "No. It's hopeless, Bette. I knew I loved you the moment my lips touched yours in the Danse au Chapelet, but I knew, too, that I must avoid you and try to thrust you out of my heart. I tried. God knows I tried!"

"But now—" I began.

"Now we have just made matters worse. You must help me, Bette. We both know that your wedding day is less than two weeks off and that nothing we can say or do will change that. If you were not King Edward's daughter— but you are. And I," he added, even more bitterly than before, "am the greatest fool in England!"

Five

I still shudder when I think of that night. How could I, a daughter of the King, have taken such risks? If Humphrey had not been watching me—indeed, if Humphrey had not been one of our party—I might well have been ravished there in the darkness. Or if he had given way to his own desires—! And, for that matter, we could so easily have been challenged by the castle guards or discovered when we were exchanging robes before I rejoined my other ladies.

None of these disasters occurred, for which I thanked God on my knees before crawling gratefully into bed. And I learned from Meg the next morning that Humphrey had hurried back into the town the moment he knew I was safe, to make sure they did not raise a hue and cry over our absence. He had, in fact, behaved toward me in such a protective fashion that my heart still warms at the memory of it.

Nor have I forgotten the way I moved through the waking hours after that terrifying evening, heavily, miserably, alive only when my eyes met Humphrey's down the supper table or when we were paired in the dance. Love, at fifteen years of age, is an all-absorbing thing; I could not—or would not—think of anything else, and my young body, awakened for the first time, ached for his touch and his kisses.

The New Year came and went, and now, with only a se'nnight remaining before my marriage, my misery mounted rapidly. Not for a moment could I thrust aside the thought of it, for each day brought more beautiful things from London that I must approve before they could be packed with the rest of my furnishings that waited to go with me to Holland: a magnificent set of gold and silver plate for my table, chapel, and kitchen; a purse with the arms of England wrought in pearls; my handsome new chariot; and what seemed like dozens of lesser items.

My bridal robes were finally finished, too, having taken thirty-five workman tailors more than four whole days and nights to make; the silver cups Meg and I had ordered for the brides in our households arrived just in time, as did a jeweled tressure I planned to wear over my coiled braids at their weddings.

The Lady Eleanore de Burgh celebrated her nuptials on January the third, and on Saturday the sixth, three days later, we followed Margaret Sackville to the church for hers. For their sakes I hid my real feelings, taking part in the dancing, singing, and other festivities with at least a pretence of merriment, and even forced myself to laugh at the usual japes and coarse jests that went on as we bedded them on their bridal nights.

Jan and I, because our own wedding day was to be on the Monday, were the butt of almost as many jokes as the brides and grooms, and it was stupid of me not to have realized that this would be so. I could so easily have excused myself earlier those evenings, but I must confess that my strongest desire, stronger than evading the teasing, was to be where I could at least see Humphrey.

Being a romantic young dreamer, I was clinging desperately to a secret hope that he would find some way to rescue me from my fate. Had he whispered in my ear that horses awaited us outside the postern gate to take us to one of remotest and least known of the de Bohun castles, I'm afraid I would have set out with him instantly.

Needless to say, he did not suggest anything so mad, and Monday morning found me standing unhappily in my bedchamber being robed for the hated ceremony that would make me foolish young Jan's wife.

Meg, equally miserable, watched from a cushioned bench, making occasional suggestions as my tiring women fastened the silver undergown, then helped me into the silken tunic that had taken so many workers so long to make. It was simple to understand why, for almost every inch was covered with exquisite embroidery and row after row of silver buttons; my girdle, which I wore low on my hips, was so heavily bejeweled that it was quite burdensome.

When these garments were arranged to everyone's satisfaction two of the tiring women lifted the long-trained mantle, lined and bordered with snowy ermine, and placed it over my shoulders, fastening it at one side of my neck. They then unbraided my hair and let it fall free, combing and smoothing it until I cried enough.

Meg rose to her feet and turned me toward a cloudy looking glass on the wall. "My b-beautiful little sister!" she said in a loving voice. "My *m-most* beautiful sister, I should say. Look at yourself, Bette—none of us has such hair. It's like a cloak of golden silk."

I eyed my reflection with distaste and said nothing. Lady Margaret, bringing in my new coronal, studded with rubies, emeralds, and pearls, echoed Meg's words as they set it carefully on my gleaming head, but I still remained silent. The fact that the glowing golden circlet matched my hair and that the sparkling emeralds made my eyes more green than blue gave me little comfort today; nothing consoled me, and I merely sighed heavily when my ladies and maids clustered around me in an admiring circle.

They then donned their own warm cloaks and we climbed down the winding staircase, Meg close beside me as we walked out into the windy courtyard. Despite the chill, bitter air it was thick with people, all pushing and shoving for a better view of us as we stepped up into my waiting chariot.

So many cooks, kitchen maids, and pantry boys came streaming around the corner of the keep that I wondered who would see that my wedding feast did not burn. Not that I cared! I waved to them when we finally set out for the church, bouncing and jolting over the rough stones and the creaking drawbridge, and continued to wave as my five horses pulled us along the streets of

Ipswich, lined, too, with cheering, smiling crowds watching us pass.

Despite their loud voices and beaming faces, my thoughts were not with them. From the moment we left the castle I was trying not to think of Humphrey, not to make everything harder for myself by wishing he were my bridegroom.

All too soon we came to a jerking halt. There, before us, was the church, surrounded by hundreds of curious townspeople, held in check by our men-at-arms. And awaiting me, flanked by the Earls of Norfolk and Hereford (Humphrey's father), stood my own sire, his face impassive, his garb a bit more sumptuous than usual, his head topping the others by several inches.

As he stepped forward to meet me, several other chariots rolled up behind mine and the rest of our ladies gathered in a quiet group, ready to follow us into the church. My maids lifted the long, weighty train of my mantle, I put my trembling hand on my father's arm, and I remember nothing more until my dear father's warm fingers were replaced by Jan's damp, shaking ones and the Bishop of London began asking us questions. We were, in fact, both shaking so much that I wonder how we remained on our feet during the ceremony and the mass that took place immediately after it. But we did, of course, and emerged from the church at last, man and wife, while the bells pealed loudly in our ears.

The crowd was still there, cheering even more lustily Whether this was for us or because several of our entourage were scattering coins among them I cannot say; probably the latter, for someone told me later that a vast sum was tossed to them that morning.

My husband said nothing until we were alone in my chariot and moving slowly back to the castle; then he drew a deep breath and gave me a hesitant smile.

"It—was a very long ceremony, my lady."

I nodded bleakly, remaining silent. After a strained moment or two he exerted himself again.

"The church was so cold. My feet are quite numb."

Turning to him, finally, I opened my mouth to reply scathingly to his empty comments, wanting, in my misery, to hurt him as much as I could. But when my eyes met his I found myself suddenly sorry for him, he looked for all the world like a cringing lost dog, expecting to be kicked or whipped. It might ease my feelings to lash out at him, I realized, but it would not make the beginning of our life together any easier.

"So are mine," I replied, trying to sound as usual. "And so are my hands. Feel them, Jan. They're like two lumps of ice!"

I heard him gulp, as I held them toward him, and saw his face flush. He took them awkwardly in his and moved closer on the jolting seat. Resisting the impulse to edge away, I left my fingers in his damp clasp all the rest of the short journey, helping him, as best I could, to break down the wall I had built up between us.

By the time we were ushered into the castle with our lords and ladies streaming after us, we were comfortable enough together to part with a smile, meeting later at the banquet table with another. I think we were both grateful that there was no need to talk; the moment we took our seats on the dais the great entertainment in our honor began, and the next few hours were occupied, while we ate my father's lavish feast, in watching hundreds of dancers, jesters, tumblers, and animals and in listening to the music of minstrels, fiddlers, harpers, and lute players.

The other tables emptied and were refilled with fresh guests. Ipswich Castle was open that day to every lord, lady, and knight; to every wealthy townsman and his good wife; to every friar, high and low, and to every member of the Carmelite order who wished to join our revels.

Long before we were free to leave our places under the elaborate canopy of state, both Jan and I were weary, and I decided that if I smelled another platter of steaming meat or fish I might be ill. But despite my tiredness and my mounting queasiness I was more than willing to remain where I was, refusing to think of the night and what it held for me.

Inevitably, however, my father rose and left the dais, leading the way himself to the wedding bedchamber. My young husband and I followed him, and all the members of our Court hurried after us, laughing and talking gaily. Meg, who was close behind me, stopped me just before we mounted the narrow stairs, lifting my fur-trimmed mantle from my aching shoulders and handing it to a maidservant to carry away.

While she was unfastening it I saw Humphrey standing in a dim corner of the corridor, watching us. My heart turned over as our eyes met, and although I tried to smile at him his own face remained white and grim. A gentle nudge from Meg broke the spell, and when I glanced back a moment later he was gone.

I remember little of the ribaldry that ensued; I was, I think, in a merciful daze. I have not forgotten, though, how quiet my dear Meg was through it all, how loving her kiss after she and the other ladies had disrobed me and helped me into the great square bed, and how closely she held my hand until Jan's friends brought him back and he climbed in beside me. Only then, bless her, did she unclasp her fingers and move away, her step lagging, the last to leave our darkened chamber.

While I listened to the sound of voices fading down the corridor, I determined to bear the ordeal facing me with courage. It was what every married woman endured.

That, certainly, was what I told myself, what I resolved. I am ashamed to admit, alas, that my good intentions melted away at Jan's first clumsy touch. I tried— but I could not hide my revulsion. There was something about his loose, wet lips and his trembling damp hands that made me cringe, and although I forced myself to lie there passively in a frozen silence, my poor young husband failed miserably in his first attempt to consummate our marriage.

I realize now how daunting my instinctive recoil and cold submission must have been to my lord, and how his shame must have mounted as he tried again and again without success. At the time, I'm afraid, I was truly glad it was so and very relieved when, at last, he crawled away to the farthest edge of our big bed and remained there.

I recall lying in the merciful dark and thinking of Meg's wedding night. *Her* young husband, she told me, had possessed her swiftly, brutally, ruthlessly, leaving her to weep into her pillow till dawn while he snored contentedly on his.

Shaken I was, to be sure, and wearied and sickened;

but *my* eyes were dry—completely dry. Then, just as drowsiness began to creep over me I heard a sound that I shall never forget; indeed, the memory of it still makes my blood run cold. It was a smothered, heartbroken sob, followed by another and then another.

Thinking, I suppose, to comfort him, I sat up and touched Jan's heaving shoulder with a tentative hand. It was, as I immediately discovered, the wrong thing to do. With an almost animal snarl he brushed my hand away.

"Leave me alone!" he cried, his voice breaking shrilly. "Oh, Mother of God, can't you leave me alone?"

Six

On went the wedding festivities, day after day, and to our marriage bed each night came my now reluctant bridegroom. Unfortunately, matters between us did not improve; indeed, they worsened so much after more shaming failures that Jan remained longer and longer every evening in the dining hall, coming to me so befuddled with wine that he would fall into a drunken sleep the moment his head rested on the pillow.

Grateful as I was for this respite, I was, at the same time, increasingly unhappy at the prospect of leaving England to spend my days among strangers and my nights beside this miserable, sodden boy. And while I lay there listening to his snores and smelling the stale wine fumes that seemed to come out of his very pores, I finally came to a decision.

The answer to my problem, I told myself, was obvious: I would simply refuse to go. After all, my father had allowed Meg to remain home, year after year. Why should I not have the same privilege? Her Jean had gone back to Brabant without her; my Jan could return to Holland without me. Why not?

Once I had made up my mind, I sought out my father at the first possible moment. Our little fleet was to sail very soon; as I remember, we were waiting for Meg's new chariot, which should have been finished long since. It was to be even more beautiful than mine, richly painted, large enough to seat five ladies, curtained in silk, all the chains gilded, and so heavy it would need six horses to pull it. Word had come from London, however, that it was finally on its way here to Ipswich, and I knew that all the final preparations for our departure were being made.

I was about to descend to the dining hall, clad in one of my loveliest robes and wearing my wedding coronal, when my father's usher hurried in to take me to his privy chamber. "His Grace will see you now, my lady," he told me. "His day has been even busier than usual."

I thought, as I knelt before him, that my father did indeed look extremely weary and that his voice sounded almost impatient as he bade me rise.

"I have only a moment to spare, my daughter," he said. "Tell me quickly what I may do for you."

The little speech I had prepared fled from my mind. "Let me remain in England with you, dear lord! I—I don't want to go with Jan!"

The minute the words left my lips I knew I should not have blurted out my request so baldly; it was, of course, too late.

"I'm sorry, Bette, but you *must* go." The lines deepened in his face, and his tones were sterner than I had ever heard them.

"No, no," I protested. "Meg didn't."

"There were reasons why Meg didn't. Your case is entirely different, my daughter, and I will not argue about it. You must go."

A feeling of desperate recklessness took possession of me, and I stared into his angry eyes. "I won't!" I said defiantly. "You cannot make me!"

He stared at me, his eyes growing even angrier. "You forget, Elizabeth, that I am the King and *you* are the King's daughter. As the King's daughter you will do whatever is expected of you, and do it with grace!"

"I will not!" I retorted hotly. "I'm flesh and blood, like anyone else. I didn't ask to be the King's daughter!"

"No, and I did not ask to be King. But I've always done my best to be worthy of the title, which, my girl, is more than you are! And as you are not, you have no right to wear that coronal."

I had seen my father in one of his rare tempers before, but never anything like this one. Before I could speak or move away he had snatched the gemmed circlet off my head and thrown it into the fire.

Without thinking, I reached into the flames, avoiding them somehow, and, just as two of the largest jewels, a ruby and an emerald, dropped down into the blazing logs, I pulled it out. As I stepped back my father gave a loud groan, and I saw that one of my wide sleeves was on fire.

In a flash he had me in his arms and had smothered the flame in his mantle. Then for a long moment he held me close, his lips on my ruffled hair.

"Bette!" I heard him whisper. "My little Bette!"

At the sound of the tenderness in his voice all my rebellious feelings melted away; I burst into tears, my arms crept up around his neck, and I burrowed my head in his shoulder.

"Forgive me, Father! Please, please forgive me. I'm so very, very sorry."

"And so am I, my child. And so am I. Come." With his arm still around me, he led me to a cushioned bench and seated me beside him. "Now that we are both a bit calmer, perhaps, I will attempt to make you understand why your demand angered me so. I have had much to bear from my family recently, and to have you speak to me thus was enough to try a saint's patience—and I am certainly no saint!"

He sighed heavily, stared into space for a moment, then began.

"First, and least important, Meg has been begging me again to allow her to remain here, which I cannot do. Indeed, I should not have been so lenient with her all these years. Next, your brother's betrothal to the Lady Philippa of Flanders is at an end, as she somehow fell into the hands of Philip of France and he refuses to release her. Added to that is the recent news that the French have driven Eleanora's husband back into Bar, so that all the gold I gave him, and the men for his campaign, have gone for naught."

He rose and walked to a window, where he stood in silence with his back to me. Then, his face even grimmer than before, he swung around and returned to my side.

"I shall now tell you, Bette, something I meant to keep to myself, for it may not be true: for some weeks I have been hearing disquieting rumors about Joanna and that squire she sent to me to be knighted—Monthermer or some such name. Yes, you may well look horrified! I keep assuring myself that no daughter of mine would fall so low as to have a liaison with a squire, but I am sufficiently concerned about these recurring stories to take her lands, goods, and chattels into my own hands until they are proven to be false. And I am, in the meantime, trying to find her a suitable new husband—possibly Amadeus of Savoy."

This final problem was, of course, the worst of all. Surely, as my father had said, it must not—it *could not* be true! And yet, even while I thought that, I remembered Humphrey's face when I asked why Joanna was not coming to my wedding. But no, *no!* It could not be true! It could not be true!

"You see, Bette," said my father, "a heavy load for a father to carry, is it not? And then for *you* to defy me, my daughter, with so little reason! Your husband is, after all, a good enough lad. He needs a firm hand, yes, but he's not like Jean of Brabant—he has no vices that I know of; we've never had any trouble with him."

"It's not that, dear Sire," I began at last. "It's—" I hesitated, not knowing how to explain, and felt the hot blood surge up into my cheeks.

"If you mean that Jan has handled you a bit roughly, Elizabeth," he said impatiently, "that is not sufficient cause for such a furor. You will soon grow accustomed— Mother of God!" he muttered almost to himself. "I should not have to discuss this with you. Surely one of your ladies—"

Realizing finally that I must, I forced myself to tell him exactly what was wrong between Jan and me, not sparing either of us in the telling. What share of the blame was mine I freely admitted to, and I made it quite clear that my lord was just as unhappy in our marriage as I was.

When I described poor Jan's desolate sobs my father sighed and patted me gently on the knee. But he said nothing until I reached the end of my sorry tale; rising, then, he strode back and forth in front of me for a short interval, his eyes thoughtful.

He returned, as he had before, and took my hand in his. "The lad is too young," he said sadly. "But how was I to know? At fifteen Meg's Jean was bedding every wench he could lay his hands on!"

While he spoke I watched him, not knowing quite what to hope for, but easier in my mind than I had been for some days. My dear sire and I were friends once more, and I was willing to do whatever he suggested.

"I can only admit that you are right, Bette," he told me now. "You and your lord would be better apart for a few months—perhaps longer. He shall sail with Margaret, just as we planned, but I will keep you with me until I go over in May. After that, my child, we will see. I may talk to Brederode about it—he's young Jan's adviser—and discuss the wisdom of you two having separate households for a year or so. But that can wait until the summer; I see no need to stir up any more trouble at the moment."

✳

The castle, when I returned to it after watching our ships sail from Harwich, was strangely quiet. All of the wedding guests were gone, their musicians and jesters with them, and the courtyard and halls were so empty and silent that I could hardly believe it was the same place.

A late supper was spread in the dining hall, but there

was nothing in the way of music or entertainment, and after eating rather sparingly I went immediately to bed. My father never appeared at all and I did not see him until the following morning, when he informed Edward and me that he was going on a pilgrimage to Our Lady of Walsingham.

"Our clergy are meeting at St. Paul's at this very moment," he told us, "to grant me, I trust, the money I need for this summer's expedition. And although I promised Canterbury that I would await his messenger at Langley, I know only too well how long-winded our men of God can be. They will, I suspect, argue the matter for many days, and I'm much too concerned over the outcome to sit there with you and twiddle my thumbs. I expect to make my pilgrimage and arrive at Langley with time to spare."

He did not suggest that I accompany him, and I found I was quite grateful. Of all our domiciles Langley, of course, was most truly my home, and my one desire at this moment was to reach it without delay, settle into its peaceful way of life, and forget, if possible, the events of the last few weeks. I wanted, among other things, to put out of my mind the picture of Meg's sad face as she bade me farewell. It was a painful scene there on the sands, although a dignified one, with our father making speeches to the assembled crowd and Jan replying in kind with one prepared for him some days earlier.

Handsome gifts were exchanged as well before the travelers departed, our father giving Meg a ring from his finger, which he placed in a square gold pyx, and bestowing on Jan a pearl-studded saddle embroidered with England's royal arms.

Meg's grief, I knew, was not because of *our* parting; we expected to meet again before long. What brought the tears into her eyes and the sob in her voice was the fear that she might never set foot on England's soil again—a fear I shared, God knows, and one I would be feeling for myself in the near future.

In the meantime, I wanted to enjoy as best I could the precious weeks at home. It was not, I soon discovered, too easy to do so. My brother and I had a miserable journey; the weather and roads were at their worst, the weeks of enforced merrymaking had exhausted us all, and every chill hour in the saddle seemed endless.

Tempers flared, our lords and ladies quarreled among themselves, the servants and men-at-arms were surly, and even my favorite little mare, usually so docile, horrified me by giving Edward's mount a nasty bite when he rode up beside me one snowy morning.

"If we ever reach Langley," I told him grimly, "I shall retire to my bedchamber and stay there for a month!"

At fifteen, however, you recover from weariness and low spirits with an amazing facility, and by the time our father joined us I was so happily settled in our old way of living that my wedding and its aftermath seemed like a bad dream.

He, too, looked less strained, and when I said as much he agreed that his journey to the small shrine at Walsingham had indeed lightened his burdens so much that he was now able to await the decision of the clergy with reasonable patience.

"But, Sire," I asked him, "if you need money for your French campaign, how can they refuse it to you?"

"By quoting the 'Clericis laicos,' Pope Boniface's most

recent bull, which forbids his clerks to pay taxes to any temporal authority. In other words, my daughter, what they are arguing right now is whether to obey their King or their Pope."

For the first time I saw how serious the matter was and, realizing just why my father was so disturbed by it, I kept my other questions to myself. How, indeed, could the clergy decide between their Pope and their King? How could anyone? And if they defied my father's commands, what would he do? There was nothing, I thought, that he *could* do!

As it happened, both Edward and I were present when the word arrived from the clerical synod, and he allowed us to remain with him while he dictated his angry reply. The message from the clergy said little, merely that after long debates all their orders had united in refusing the King's request for money.

He read it aloud to us, then dismissed the clerk who had carried it, his ire showing plainly in his face and voice.

"Remain in the castle until I summon you again," he said. "I will give you a reply to this—letter—to take back to your masters."

After the timid-looking man had bowed his way out, my brother and I watched our father pace up and down the chamber, deep in thought. We were seated together in a window embrasure, where we had been playing a game of merels, and we now kept very quiet, hoping that he would not dismiss us, too.

"My scribe," he said suddenly. "I want him here immediately." Then he turned to us. "As I have discussed this problem with both of you," he said, "you may stay and hear my answer."

Until his bowlegged, red-nosed secretary scurried in, he continued to pace the floor. When the scribe was seated and had his pen in his hand, our father spoke abruptly to him.

"First, a letter to the synod at St. Paul's. No greetings. Begin thus: 'Since you do not observe the homage and fealty you have sworn to me, I, too, will not be bound to you in anything. No clerk shall be allowed to sue in my Courts; such of the Church's lands as are held by ordinary lay tenures shall be taken into my hands; and henceforward any layman meeting a monk or clerk riding a better horse than his may lawfully appropriate it to his own use. I do, in fact, hereby declare that the whole Clerical Estate is put out of the law.' "

I heard my brother gasp. Young as he was, even Edward could tell what a drastic step our sire was taking. I must confess that it quite frightened me, and I did not dare even whisper to Edward while our father dictated a public proclamation in which he used many of the same phrases that were in his letter.

After he had finished, he came over to where we were sitting and spoke directly to my young brother.

"You heard, my son? A King is forced to make many difficult decisions during his reign, and this particular one has been very, very hard!" He sighed heavily. "But if I am to continue ruling England, I must be strong—and sure. And think first and always of my country. Remember this, and remember today when it is your turn to wear the Crown. England *must* come first!"

Seven

*I*t was early February and we were still all at Langley when a fresh rumor reached our ears concerning Joanna and Ralph de Monthermer. She had moved her household to Caerphilly Castle, a stronghold in faraway mountainous Glamorganshire so ringed in by marshes that it discouraged visitors, but a few neighbors who had ventured in to make her welcome were talking freely of the unseemly intimacy that appeared to exist between the King's daughter and her erstwhile squire.

After hearing this my father exploded in another burst of wrath, for which, I must say, none of us could blame him. What *could* Joanna be thinking of to so besmirch her name and ours?

"If Amadeus of Savoy learns of this he will refuse to

wed her," he said to me. "I would, in his place. As you know, Bette, I've sent letter after letter to Joanna inquiring into this matter, and her replies tell me nothing—nothing! Just one evasion after another. I'm afraid I must go to Wales myself."

For the next few days my brother Edward and I saw little of him, as he was too occupied preparing for his journey to Caerphilly to take his meals in the dining hall or to allow us the freedom of his privy chamber. There were so many matters to be settled before he could absent himself that the road to London was filled with royal couriers coming and going every day; the sound of trumpets and horses' hooves in the courtyard became constant; crowds of strangers thronged the corridors, awaiting permission to bring pressing business to their King's attention; and we were told that travelers could not find a bed in our vicinity for any amount of money.

Everything was confusion. Before long I retired to my own apartments, leaving them only to ride for an hour or so in the pleasantest part of the day or to visit Edward in his. Sometimes he supped with me; sometimes I supped with him; often I shared a simple meal with my ladies and went early to bed, only to be kept awake until the small hours by the unusual noise and bustle.

On the morning before my father's departure, discovering that the weather had turned warm, I decided to join my brother's hawking party. I was just mounting my mare when Edward, already in his saddle, gave an exclamation of surprise and walked his horse nearer mine.

"Can I be seeing aright, Bette? On that mule—there, coming through the gate—is that not my lord of Canterbury? Archbishop Winchelsea? On a mule?

Looking to where he was pointing, I realized why he sounded so astonished. There could be no doubt that it was his Grace—that great belly alone was unmistakable—and although I had rarely talked with him (he shunned women except in the confessional), I had been in his presence often enough to recognize him even at a distance.

But, as Edward had said, why on a mule? He was known to be unusually affable and easy with his inferiors, to be sure, but when he appeared in public it was always as my lord of Canterbury, with all the pomp and precedence of his high office.

A hasty glance around the courtyard told me that our steward and ushers must all be occupied elsewhere. A word to Edward was sufficient; trotting immediately to the Archbishop's side he dismounted, helped his Grace down from his undignified beast, talked with him for a few minutes, then led him inside the castle.

In the meantime, for not much of the February sunshine reached us in the walled courtyard, we walked our horses back and forth to keep them warm. Edward was not gone long, however, and we were soon trotting out over the drawbridge and heading for the open countryside. He said nothing until we halted and began unhooding our birds. Then, taking advantage of a moment when no one else was close, he told me that his Grace had hurried from London hoping to make peace with our father, and on the way he and his entourage had had their horses seized by some of our royal officers.

"A villager provided him with that mule," said Edward, his eyes dancing, "but the rest of his party may never reach here at all!"

It was, of course, just the kind of incident to delight a

boy of thirteen, and he chuckled over it for hours. But it seemed to me that it might well add to the trouble between the clergy and our father, and I found it difficult to join in his mirth.

Later we heard from our father himself that their interview had been a stormy one, and that the Archbishop had failed in his mission.

"Unfortunately," he told us, "our forces in Gascony have suffered a severe defeat. Winchelsea and the rest of the clergy insist that this is the finger of Providence, punishing me for placing them outside the law. A handy weapon to use in bending me to their will, I must admit, but I remained firm and gave them only until Easter to submit to my demands."

"And if they still refuse? What then, sir?"

"Then, my son, I will confiscate the whole of their lands."

Edward whistled softly. "A grim reply to carry back to St. Paul's! I do not envy my lord of Canterbury."

"I am not to be envied either, Edward, for this defeat in Gascony means I must send our forces there immediate assistance—adopt a new plan altogether. In fact, the moment de Bohun returns from Brabant I shall summon our nobles to Salisbury to ask their aid Our leading earls will, I trust, be willing to go without me to Gascony while I sail to Flanders to rouse our friends there."

My heart sank. Flanders! So soon! But one look at his set face was enough to still the protest that leaped to my lips.

"Well," he continued in a weary voice, "this is the end of my plan to visit Joanna. I shall send Walter de Winterborn in my place."

I shivered for my sister. Our father's confessor would stand for no evasions; if there was any truth in the rumors we had heard he would ferret it out swiftly and implacably, and daughterly tears would avail her nothing.

They were not to help me, either, from this day on, as I was soon to discover. A courier came to us from Holland to inform us of the prosperous voyage and safe arrival there of my lord husband, and my father, after thanking him, called for the royal purse and gave him ten shillings.

"For bringing us such good tidings," he said, then turned and looked meaningfully at me.

I'm ashamed to confess that I stared back at him as if I did not understand what he meant. At the moment I did not care whether my husband had had a prosperous voyage or not, and I saw no reason why I should give any of *my* money to his messenger. My eyes were the first to fall, however, and, well aware that my father was still looking at me, I began to feel uncomfortable.

"Well, my daughter?"

I glanced up, pretending innocent bewilderment. "My lord?" I asked in a small voice.

"You have your purse on your girdle, I see."

"Oh—yes." Slowly and grudgingly, I opened it and drew out ten shillings as he had.

"No."

I drew out another ten.

"No, Elizabeth." There was such sternness now in the quiet way he said those two words that my defiance melted and I hastily made the sum fifty shillings, forcing myself to smile and thank the courier as I placed it in his hand.

That was the last time my father spoke to me that evening, and his chill nod when I bade him good night sent me to bed in a guilty, unhappy mood. Determined to make my peace with him, I rose early the following morning and set out for his privy chamber.

On the way I encountered Edward, who informed me that I might as well return to my own apartments.

"He's keeping two scribes busy, summoning our nobles to a Parliament at Salisbury. It seems that de Bohun reached home on the same ship that brought Jan's courier to us, so he need wait no longer to assemble them. From what his usher told me, I doubt that either of us will see our father before he sets out himself for Salisbury."

I watched him run off to join his young companions, my heart heavy and my spirits low. I was not accustomed to being in my father's bad graces and I disliked it excessively, finding it more and more difficult to excuse my foolish behavior. When he did not join us all at supper, I left the hall as soon as I could and hurried again to his privy chamber.

The guard at the door looked at me with surprise, but before he could question my unannounced entry I was inside. Except for my dear sire, seated before a simple repast of bread and cold meat, the chamber was empty. As he reached for his flagon of wine his eyes fell on me, standing quietly just over the threshold.

He must have known from my face what I was feeling, for he rose and held out his arms. I flew into them, sobbing out my apologies and telling him, disjointedly, how miserable I had been all night and all day. What he replied I do not remember, but I left his presence swearing to myself that I would behave more seemingly in the future.

✳

February ended and March blustered in without any word from Salisbury. Welcoming, as I did, any postponement of the day when I must leave England, I was very glad to have it so and was actually quite relieved, one morning, when the clatter and bustle of someone arriving in the courtyard was *not* a messenger from my father.

Instead, it was our kinswoman Isabella de Vescy, safely home after accompanying Meg to Brabant. A cousin of our mother, she had become, in 1280, the second wife of one of my father's most trusted barons and, nine years later, his widow. Soon after her husband's death she joined Meg's household and before long was loved dearly by us all.

I know that the sight of her sweet face cheered me instantly on this chill, rainy day, although her news of my sister was not too happy.

"I left her in good health," she told us, "but far from content. Her lord received her with the cordiality proper to the occasion, behaving fairly well for a few days. Then, as I suppose was only to be expected, he relapsed into his usual way of life and we saw little of him." She shook her head. "Our parting was sad; however, we kept reminding each other that we would meet soon again when I cross the water with *you*, my dear child."

"Perhaps not so very soon," I replied, telling her of my father's latest problems. "And much as I want to see Meg, Lady Isabella, I cannot help hoping it will be late rather than soon!"

As she was now a member of my household, she settled down with us at Langley and so was present when Walter de Winterborn returned from Wales. Joanna, he told us, was not at Caerphilly, nor could he discover from her people where she had gone.

"I rode from castle to castle seeking word of her where-abouts," he continued wearily, "but without the least success. So here I am, not knowing how to tell my lord King of her strange absence."

Rather hesitantly I asked him whether Ralph De Monthermer was with her when she left to Caerphilly.

"He was. Apparently they set out to 'attend to urgent family business and might not return for some weeks'—or so they told her household there."

"And the children?"

"Her small daughters are with her, not young Gilbert."

Not having anything to suggest, we encouraged Walter to hurry on to Salisbury to inform my father. Joanna's disappearance was indeed worrying, but there might, as Lady Isabella said hopefully, be some innocent explanation.

We had not thought of any, though, when, some days later, we were discussing the matter over our needlework. It was a gray, ugly morning, so chill that I had refused my brother's invitation to hawk with him and his young companions. Three of my ladies decided to brave the cold and joined his party; the others, seeing me settled by the fire with Lady Isabella, took advantage of this lull in our usual activities to busy themselves elsewhere.

As a result, my kinswoman and I were alone in my privy chamber with no one nearby but a tiring woman in the adjoining room. Our usher entered without warning, followed by a tall, thin priest, whose face was all but hidden in the hood of his thick cloak.

"If you please, my lady," said my usher, "I have here the Lady Joanna's chaplain, who insisted on coming to you immediately."

"Before I could reply, our visitor stepped forward and threw back his hood. It was indeed Robert Bareback, my sister's chaplain, a man we all knew very well, for he had been the clerk of her chapel for as long as I could remember.

"Forgive me, my daughter," he began as I rose to welcome him. "I would not have intruded thus had I not needed to see you in private and without delay.

While he was speaking Lady Isabella rose, too, and placed her canvas and silks on a low chest. "No, no," I protested, seeing her begin to move toward the door. "Stay with us, Cousin. We have no secrets from the Lady Isabella," I said hastily to Robert Bareback. "This is our cousin, the Lady Isabella de Vescy, Father. Whatever you have to tell me I would like her to hear."

"I bring you a letter," was all he said, handing it to me.

I saw, as I unrolled the parchment, that it could hardly be called a letter. It was too short. *If you love me*, Joanna had scrawled, *come to me at Goodrich Castle. I need a sister's help*.

My first feeling was relief—great relief. Goodrich Castle was the favorite home of my sister Joanna's godmother (another kinswoman), the dowager Countess of Pembroke, mother of Aymar de Valence; Joanna had not, as I had secretly feared, run off to some remote hideaway with her lowborn squire!

I showed the short note to Lady Isabella, then urged Robert Bareback to tell us just why Joanna had sent for me. He refused, saying that his mistress wished to inform me herself.

"But I do assure you, my lady, that her need is truly pressing, or I would not have come to you here, knowing as I do that the King is in Salisbury and I would find you alone. Riding around the country on a clandestine errand is distasteful to me, and I go even further against my conscience when I suggest, as I now do, that we set out immediately, telling no one here what is your destination."

For a moment I stared at him, appalled. Lady Isabella did the same. Then, seeing the grave concern on my sister's chaplain's face, I asked him no more questions. Instead, I turned to Lady Isabella.

"Will you come with me? Your presence would make it possible for me to agree to Joanna's proposal." It flashed into my mind that Goodrich Castle was not far from Humphrey's home in Hereford, but I did not let myself linger on that thought.

Lady Isabella sighed. "Oh, dear! Well, I cannot allow you to go alone, dear child. But I must confess that, like you, Father Bareback, I find such a clandestine journey distasteful."

He nodded. "I will only repeat, ladies, that my mistress needs you."

On looking back over our journey, I remember being astonished at how many miles our small entourage could ride in a day and how well both Robert Bareback and Lady Isabella stood the long hours in the saddle and the miserable weather that dogged us at first. Before we reached Gloucestershire, however, the skies cleared, the air softened, and, here and there along the way, we began to see the flowers that herald springtime.

Having put ourselves in the care and guidance of Joanna's chaplain, we did not question his decision, each night, to seek shelter in small, quiet hostels. It was apparent that he hoped no one would recognize me, and, as we were traveling with only a tiring woman and a few men-at-arms, clothed in our warmest but plainest garments, there was no reason why anyone would. For this same reason we passed our last night on the road at an abbey near Painswick instead of nearby Gloucester Castle, and this time Robert told us why.

"My lady does not want her people there to know that she is at Goodrich—not yet, I should say. For the moment she is keeping her whereabouts secret from them, too."

His words brought all my own questions to my lips, where they had hovered from the day he arrived at Langley. Again I forced them back, assuring myself that I would very soon hear the answers from Joanna.

To Robert's great relief the abbot was absent, and we entered the sprawling old building in its deep hollow as casual wayfarers, then left it early the following morning in the same manner, having eaten a simple repast of bread and cheese shortly after daybreak.

By riding across the countryside we avoided Gloucester entirely, fording the Severn at its narrowest point and making our way through the quiet beeches, conifers, and oaks of the Forest of Dean, one of our royal woodlands. I cannot describe the beauty and peace of that lovely spot: the huge trees, the dappled patterns made by the March sun filtering through their leaves, the glossy ivy, the patches of purple violets—and, underfoot, the fallen needles of the fir trees, cushioning the *clop-clop* of our horses' hooves.

For the last few miles we followed the curving Wye, halting finally at a small stone maison-dieu on its southern bank. The cross on its roof told us it was a pilgrim hostel, and the de Valence arms, cut into the front wall, that we were now on Pembroke land. Close beside it stood a ferry and, as it took us across the river, we found ourselves gazing up at a steep escarpment that rose from the farther bank; the castle, according to the ferryman, was out of sight on its top.

"Follow that trail," he said, pointing the way.

We obeyed, our weary mounts snorting and shaking their heads as the narrow pathway soon grew almost perpendicular. Slowly, slowly, we climbed, so shut in by trees that we could see nothing but the trail ahead of us; up and up, up and up—I learned later that although the sheer side of the hill was only one hundred feet high, that trail on its southern slope wound for at least a half mile and seemed twice the distance.

Then, suddenly, we were there, out of the trees and in the open, staring at what I still consider the most magnificent castle I have ever seen. And I have seen many! I know I gave an audible gasp of admiration when we reined in our horses, who, poor beasts, were sweating and panting from the steep ascent.

Perhaps it was the unusual color of the huge pile that made it so unforgettable; it had all been fashioned of a rosy red stone, rising majestically out of rocks of the same warm tone. Or perhaps it was the superb situation, the high windswept plateau with its glorious spread of countryside below.

Joanna's chaplain, close beside me, gave a gentle laugh. "It takes one's breath away, does it not? A most remarkable sight."

"Building up here must have been a great feat," I said "The very thought frightens me."

"Much of it was erected not long ago by the late Earl,"

he replied. "The Countess will, I am sure, be happy to tell you all about it. As you see, they used the native stone, cut here on the hilltop. But come, my lady, we must not linger. Our friends at the castle will have seen us approach and will be waiting for us."

This, apparently, was true. The drawbridge was down, the portcullis raised, voices from the gatehouse hailed us as we rode into the inner bailey, and, as we crossed the courtyard to the range of buildings on the northern side that Robert told us housed the great hall and solar, I saw a cluster of ladies gathered in the open doorway.

Lady Joanna, the handsome gray-haired Countess of Pembroke for whom our Joanna was named, came forward to meet me the moment my feet touched the cobbles; but, although I searched for it, my sister's dark head was nowhere visible. There were many faces staring down at us from the arched windows in the red stone walls, and chattering groups of servants lurked in the corridors to watch us pass. But where, oh, where, was Joanna?

"My dear goddaughter awaits you in her chamber," said the Countess, leading us up the stairs. "I will take you to her immediately, Elizabeth, while you, Lady Isabella, wash away the dust before supper."

Her expression was so grave, her brown eyes so strained that I began to feel frightened. For the first time a dreadful thought occurred to me: Joanna was ill, suffering from some strange disorder, or—worse—she had gone mad!

We had never had that particular trouble in our family, but we had friends with elderly aunts who had to be hidden away, young mothers fallen into melancholy, men and women grown violent at certain times in their lives.

Could this be the reason why Joanna had come here

secretly without telling even her people where she was going? Was Ralph de Monthermer her keeper, chosen perhaps by her chaplain to protect her from herself?

I so terrified myself with these new fears that, when my hostess pointed out the doorway to Joanna's chamber and hurried off, I could hardly enter it. With a pounding heart and trembling legs, however, I crossed the threshold.

"Bette?" My sister's voice reached me now, setting the worst of my imaginings at rest, and I moved swiftly toward her, calling myself a fool. She was standing with her back to the light, her arms outstretched. I ran into them and, as we kissed each other warmly, I knew instantly why she had chosen to greet me here, and alone.

Joanna was heavy with child.

Eight

$\mathcal{I}$ think I gasped. I remember Joanna releasing me and moving a little away.

"I know what you are thinking, Bette," she said, trying to smile. "So I hasten to tell you that part of it is not true! I am wed to the father of the child in my womb."

Stunned and completely unable to reply, I simply stood there, staring at her. Joanna married? But—

After a moment she shrugged her shoulders and gave a bitter laugh. "I suppose I was a fool to expect a warm response from you simply because you are my sister. You look even more horrified than did my godmother when I told her."

"But I don't see how you *can* be married, Jo," I protested, finding my tongue at last. "None of us can wed without our father's consent; you know that as well as I do. How would *you* look if I suddenly announced such a thing to you?"

"I think I might show some concern for you, an attempt to understand—"

"Understand *what?* Surely the fact that I hurried here to you the moment you sent for me is proof enough of my concern. But you must see that I cannot understand something I know nothing about." I went to her, then, and put my arms around her. "Be reasonable, Jo! Tell me what has happened and why you wanted me here."

She nodded. "You are right, Bette. Forgive me for turning on you so, but I've been frantic—frantic! Of course you know nothing. How could you? Nothing, I mean, that has occurred since Gilbert's death. It was no secret that we were miserably unhappy together, however; you and everyone else were aware of that."

"We were, yes. But you have three children, Jo!"

"As you say, I have three children—and I love them dearly. But I happen to need more in my life than just children. I understand that many women do not; *you* may not. If you are lucky, being a mother will keep you content and happy. I wish it did me, but unfortunately it does not. You see, Bette, I need a man's love also."

While she was talking I was thinking that I, too, would like a man's love, and so, I was sure, would Meg. And Mary. What woman would not? None of us could expect it, however, or demand it, for we, alas, were the King's daughters. As was Jo.

"I remember our mother saying, 'No matter how or what we feel, the King's family must always think first of England's good,' " I said.

"And so I did, for six interminable years. For six years I belonged body and soul to a man I loathed, bore him three children, shivered through grim winters in his bleak, bitterly cold castles, wishing I had never been born. Is that not enough, Bette? Could anyone expect me to sacrifice myself a second time and give up a lover with whom I have found more happiness than I ever imagined existed?"

An expression came over her face, as she spoke, that I had never seen there before, half agonized, half rapturous.

"God knows I fought my love for him," she went on. "I'm not a fool, nor is he. We knew the dangers and we planned to part, but suddenly our love was too strong—or we were too weak—and even before I discovered I was with child I knew that no matter what the price I could not live without Rafe."

Rafe. She had finally answered the question I dared not ask. So all the rumors were true, then? A daughter of the King had stooped to a common squire.

"Was that when you asked our father to knight him?" I asked, almost sure of what she would reply.

She nodded. "But not just because I loved him, you understand," she added defensively. "My lord is more worthy of knighthood than half those who wear the spurs. And Gilbert would have said the same, I know, for he often told me Rafe was the one member of our household on whom he could lean and trust. As I discovered later for myself. Nothing, Bette, was too much for him to do for me; no problem too difficult to solve, no burden too heavy for his shoulders. And he asked for so little—just to be our squire."

Staring dreamily into space, she was silent for a moment.

"Finally I sent him to our father and he came back to me

Sir Ralph de Monthermer. What a happy day—what a happy day!"

"You were too happy to leave him, I suppose, and come to my wedding. We were all wondering, of course."

"By the middle of December I was sure I was *enceinte*, Bette, and too frightened to come to Ipswich or face anyone. I could not sleep nights, and my days were almost as bad."

"It must have been then that word about you reached our father. I don't know who carried the tale, Jo, but some story came to his ears."

Joanna smiled wryly. "As I soon learned. Did he tell you that he wrested almost all of my possessions from me, leaving me not penniless, perhaps, but with barely enough for myself and my children?"

"No, all he said to me was that he was arranging a marriage for you with the Earl of Savoy."

"That was some weeks later. First his escheators came to every one of my castles bearing a royal mandate from him at Castle Acre, ordering them, for reasons unspecified, to take into their hands my lands, goods, and chattels and to keep them safely until they should hear to the contrary —'as they valued their safety and would avoid the King's indignation!' And, oh, Bette, he referred to me as the Countess of Gloucester instead of 'the dearest daughter of the King.' "

I must confess that, remembering our father's other troubles, including my own rebellion, I was not surprised that he had acted thus. In fact, I was about to relate his side of the matter when Jo went on with her story and I remained silent, deciding to tell her later how, at that particular time, he was beset on all sides.

"Most of my people obeyed the mandate instantly," I heard her continue. "Except my brave and loyal Luke de Gare, who refused to yield up my castle at Tunbridge. They seized everything he owned and forced him and his son to face our father's wrath in person."

"I know nothing of that," I replied. "However, I *was* with him when he despatched Walter de Winterborn to Caerphilly to question you about the unsavory rumors concerning you and your Rafe, and I was still at Langley when Walter returned, having failed to find you. By then, of course, our father had journeyed on to Salisbury for the meeting of Parliament, where we sent Walter immediately."

"I had come here to Goodrich Castle on the fourteenth day of February," Joanna explained. "Rafe and I were secretly married in early January, and I knew I must not delay too long before informing our father. Robert Bareback went to fetch you; I sent for Gilbert, who is here now, Bette; and I brought little Elizabeth and Margaret with me."

I had seen Gilbert, now six years old, when his parents took him to Court, but their small daughters had never left Wales before, and as I was expressing my delight at the prospect of meeting my godchild, we heard a scratch on the door. I saw Joanna turn a lovely pink and her dark eyes soften. "It's my lord," she told me. "I asked him to give us some time alone before joining me here."

All I remembered of the young squire who had come to Court to be knighted was that he had a pleasing countenance and was unusually well-mannered for someone of low birth. To my great surprise and relief, the man striding into Joanna's chamber looked more the gentleman than either my husband or Margaret's. There was an air of assurance about him, too, which made me understand why he had been of such assistance to Jo, and when he took her hand in his and smiled into her eyes I could almost feel the love flowing between them.

His eyes were hazel, I noticed, deeply set and wide apart; his hair a tawny brown; and I thought, as I watched him smile, that his mouth was the mouth of a man who was no stranger to suffering and discipline.

Picturing my vacuous young Jan and Meg's fat Jean, I suddenly found myself envying Jo despite the difficulties ahead for her. To be loved by Ralph de Monthermer—squire, knight, or nobleman—was to be a fortunate woman indeed.

She led him to me and he bent over my hand. "I have come a long way to meet you, brother Rafe," I said warmly, "and to help you and Joanna in any way I can. Command me, if you will."

"God bless you, my lady!" he replied fervently, lifting my fingers to his lips. "I need not tell you how desperate our situation or how greatly I blame myself for placing my beloved wife in this plight. You are King Edward's youngest and favorite daughter. Soften his wrath toward my lady, and I will be forever grateful."

I did not say what I was thinking—that he had set me an impossible task—and by common consent we delayed any further discussion of the matter until the following day. We supped quietly together, passed a pleasant evening, and retired early to bed. After a restful night I returned to Joanna's apartments, this time to renew my acquaintance with her son and to meet my two little nieces.

I had never spent much time with small children (since

I ceased being one myself), and I must confess that my interest in my namesake was more because she was my one and only goddaughter than for any other reason. On our way to their quarters I asked Jo whether Elizabeth resembled her or her father.

Jo laughed. "Neither of us, Bette, although she has Gilbert's red hair. Wait until you see her. I will tell you this: it is obvious that she belongs to our family."

There seemed, at first glance, to be a roomful of laughing and squealing young things. Some game was in progress which halted abruptly at our entrance, and in the silence that fell I saw that there were only the three I expected to find there, a thin-legged lad with Joanna's dark eyes and two tiny redheaded girls.

Before anyone could say anything, the smaller one lifted the skirt of her long gown and ran unsteadily toward us. She came directly to me, dropping her robe when she reached my feet to hold out her plump arms. As I leaned down to gather her into mine, she gave a gurgle of delight and I found myself looking into a face so much like mine that I could hardly believe it.

With another gurgle she clasped me around the neck and nestled her red curls into my shoulder. A new and pleasant feeling swept over me, and I realized that I was wishing with all my heart that this enchanting armful of babyhood was my own daughter, not just my goddaughter.

On impulse I carried her to where a sheet of polished metal hung on the rough stone wall and called to Joanna to come and see our two faces reflected in it side by side.

Laughing again, she obeyed. "I know, Bette. It's almost ridiculous, isn't it? From the time she was a year old she has been so much like you that I could hardly wait for this moment. And to think that she is the one we named for you! Now put her down and meet my little Margaret—who doesn't resemble Meg in the least, as you will see."

Long after we returned to Joanna's apartments I continued to think about the joy I had felt in holding Elizabeth in my arms, and after I went to bed that night I remembered it again. If Jan and I could have such a child, I told myself, my future would not be so empty after all; and I fell asleep resolving that when I joined my young husband in Holland I would do my part—or more than my part, if necessary—to make our marriage a true one.

I should, of course, have been trying to solve Jo's problem instead of dwelling on my private concerns. We had spent a goodly portion of the day discussing it, first by ourselves and then with Rafe, Lady Joanna, and our dear Lady Isabella, who joined us in Jo's privy chamber. None of us, however, had anything very helpful to suggest, agreeing finally that we should not approach my father until he had dissolved Parliament.

After this fairly fruitless talk I settled down to enjoy this peaceful interval, hoping in my secret heart to see or hear something of Humphrey but never finding the right moment to inquire whether he was now at Hereford Castle, which lay about fifteen miles away. With each day that passed the weather grew more settled and the countryside more beautiful, and before long we were spending much of them outside the great redstone castle walls, never very far away, to be sure, but exploring comfortably the softly greening banks of the river at the foot of our steep hill.

On many of these small expeditions we took the children, delighting them by eating our nooning beside the swiftly running water; and as I watched them frolicking with Joanna and Rafe I decided that, no matter what our father said or did about their secret marriage, Jo had been right in wedding the man she loved. Even if he stripped her of all her titles and perquisites, she would have more to make her happy than I could hope for with my weakling husband.

We had at least a week of uninterrupted pleasure, seeing no one but ourselves and the members of the Pembroke household, knowing nothing of what was happening in the outside world. We rose, one morning, to find the sun shining brightly and, even there on our high hilltop, very little wind. I wandered out into the castle green, holding a small maiden by each hand, and after we had made our daily visit to watch the swallows building their nests in the arches of our solar windows, the red clay that they carried there in their beaks so much the color of the stone that, at a casual glance, the round additions seemed a part of the carving, the children begged me to take them to the river again.

Joanna and Rafe and the older ladies were more than willing, and we were all soon on our steep descent through the trees. When we reached the bottom we halted for a moment, discussing whether to follow the Wye to the left, until we came to the beautiful stretch of glades and grassy banks that we saw from the windows of the solar, looking north over the outer ward walls, or perhaps, for a change, to the right.

While we talked the skies clouded over and we had a new decision to make. The sensible thing, of course, was to return immediately to the castle, but this brought wails of disappointment from the children.

It was Rafe who settled the problem to everyone's satisfaction. He pointed to the castle ferry, tied to a tree a few yards away, and to the small stone maison-dieu—our pilgrims' inn—on the other side of the river. "We'll remain near enough to the ferry," he said, "so that we can seek shelter in the inn if it rains heavily."

By the time we were settled in a pretty spot that was hidden from the ferry by a stand of trees, the sun was out again and there seemed no reason to hurry our meal. The servants began to unpack the baskets, spreading the contents on the grass, and as young Gilbert and Margaret were soon busy with a pair of small fishing rods made for them by their stepfather, I took my namesake off to pick a bunch of violets for her mother.

Our search led us back the way we had come, for I remembered noticing a thick patch of their heart-shaped leaves in the copse that lay between our resting place and the ferry. We were both bending over it, plucking the delicate purple-blue blossoms, when the sound of a horse's hooves on wood caught my attention. A step or two took me to the edge of the trees, and I saw that the flat-bottomed skiff was carrying a man and his mount toward our side of the river.

Stepping out, he led his spirited black stallion ashore. Before he could jump into the saddle Elizabeth ran past me to him, leaving a trail of violets behind her, her plump little hands outstretched. He quickly tied his horse to a tree and came to meet her; as he caught her up into his arms I realized that it was Humphrey. I remained where I was, watching the pretty scene, my heart pounding. He tossed her in the air once or twice, which set her gurgling, then suddenly held her off and stared into her face, looking startled.

I chose that moment to emerge from my hiding place, smothering a sigh as I did so. Why, I asked myself, could this not be my small daughter and Humphrey her proud and happy father? I don't know whether he shared my thought, but he kissed her before he put her down, then took her hand and led her back to me.

"I rode down from Hereford, my lady," he said in greeting, "having heard a rumor that you and the Lady Joanna were here at Goodrich. But no one told me I would find two of you!"

"She's Jo's youngest, my namesake and goddaughter."

"I've never seen such a resemblance. I dare not tell you what I felt when I saw her face!"

There being nothing I could say to that, I fell silent, and for a moment or two so did he. I wanted to be in his arms of course, but that was now impossible—doubly impossible. The longing was so great, however, that I could think of nothing else, and it was not until I heard Rafe's voice, calling my name, that I awoke to the awkwardness facing me. Humphrey, I was sure, did not know of Joanna's situation. What was I to do?

Nine

Fortunately, I had to do nothing. While I hesitated, young Gilbert came out of the copse, followed by his mother.

Jo, obviously startled at finding Humphrey with me, gave a little gasp, then greeted him in a slightly strained voice. I saw his eyes widen, the outline of her thickened body apparent even in its soft robe.

"If you are looking for Aymar de Valence," she said, "he is at Salisbury with the other nobles."

"That I know," was Humphrey's reply, "for he journeyed there with my father's entourage. No, my lady, I rode over because we heard that you and the Lady Elizabeth were at Goodrich. I bring affectionate greetings from my mother, who urges you both to come to her at Hereford before you leave this part of the country. She has not been well the last few months or she would have accompanied me today."

I remained silent, thinking it best for Joanna to do the talking. After expressing polite concern over our Aunt Maud's ill health, she turned to me.

"Take the children back to the others, if you will, Bette. My lord Humphrey and I will join you shortly."

As we strolled through the woods, we met Rafe coming to see where everyone had disappeared to in such a mysterious fashion.

"First you and Elizabeth," he said, "and then my lady and Gilbert!"

When I told what had happened he groaned.

"I suppose we should have expected this," he commented in a resigned voice. "How could we hope to hide the presence of *two* of the King's daughters at Goodrich? Well, my lady and his lordship are old friends. She will know what to tell him."

Remembering the odd look on Humphrey's face when, so many months ago now, he brought me Jo's wedding gift and informed me that she would not be coming to Ipswich, I decided that he knew at least part of her story already. She was probably telling him of her secret marriage, and, perhaps, pledging him to secrecy.

I learned later that this was so. They appeared in a few minutes, chatting easily together, and after Humphrey had greeted our Lady Isabella, the Countess of Pembroke, and Rafe, we all settled down to eat the tempting viands prepared for us on the grassy riverbank. Nothing was said of Joanna's problem, of course, and Humphrey, perhaps to make her forget her anxieties for an hour or two, exerted himself to amuse our small party with a skill I did not know he possessed.

For me it was a golden interlude. Even now I can feel the sun on our faces and hear Jo and Rafe laughing together; I can see the children playing on the greensward and the two older ladies napping contentedly on piles of cushions nearby; and I remember as if it were yesterday the warmth that flooded over me when, as they very often did, Humphrey's eyes sought mine. We had no time alone but this was fortunate, for it would have availed us nothing—merely stirring up fires that must better remain banked.

Much too soon the shadows lengthened and the best of the day was gone. We returned to the road and, after starting the rest of our group up the steep hill to the castle, Joanna, Rafe, and I lingered for a few minutes to say farewell to Humphrey.

"You will make our excuses to Aunt Maud," said Jo. "Tell her, if need be, why I stay in seclusion here, and that my next journey must certainly be to join the King and seek his recognition of my marriage. That, we all agree, should wait until Parliament is dissolved."

"Which will be soon, I think," replied Humphrey, nodding his head. "We expect my father home any day now."

"In the meantime," my sister told him, "come to us whenever you can."

✳

Humphrey's visit marked the end of both the fair weather and our peace of mind. It began raining late that night, and, although there were a few sunny intervals in the week that followed, it was too wet and chilly for us to

venture outside the castle walls even if we had so desired—
which I, for one, did not, hoping that Humphrey would
accept Jo's invitation to join us again. And Jo, I knew, was
becoming more and more restless as each day passed, eager
now to face her ordeal and have it over.

Any unusual activity in the courtyard would take me
running to the nearest window that overlooked it, thinking
it might be either Humphrey or Aymar. When they *did*
arrive they came together, and I, happening to be in a most
remote corner of the solar tower playing with the children,
had no idea why Joanna wanted me to come to her.

I hastened in, not waiting to tidy either my hair or gown,
both of which were in wild disarray from one of little
Elizabeth's games, and I was across the threshold before I
realized that she and the other ladies were not alone. I
think I took a step backwards; then I saw Aymar's unmistakable long thin face, dominated by its large hooked nose,
and, standing just behind him, Humphrey.

Forgetting my appearance, I hurried across the chamber
to greet them. They both looked so grim, however, that I
barely waited for them to respond.

"Something has happened," I heard myself say in a
frightened voice. "I see it in your faces."

"I am afraid you are right," replied Aymar. "Humphrey's father and the Earl of Norfolk have quarreled seriously with King Edward, and Parliament dissolved in
what I can only describe as disorder."

My heart sank. First the clergy, now my father's two
most powerful nobles! Where was it going to end? And
how, with this fresh burden, could my sister add hers?

I glanced at her and saw that her face was white. "Sit
down, Bette," she told me in a harsh, despairing voice.

"Aymar has been waiting to tell us just what occurred'

I obeyed, choosing a cushioned stool between Aymar's mother and the Lady Isabella, noticing, as I did so, that none of our other ladies were present. They had been sent away, I assumed, so that Aymar might speak freely.

He proceeded to do so, leaving nothing to our imaginations. The cause of the quarrel, he told us, was that because our father's own expedition was still delayed he had ordered his nobles to set out for Gascony immediately and begin the campaign against the French without him.

"This my lords of Hereford and Norfolk refused to do, arguing that as England's Marshal and Constable they were bound to attend the King in person. Norfolk was very eloquent and very firm. 'Willingly will I go with you, Sire,' he replied before us all, 'and fight in the first line of battle, which is my hereditary duty—'

" 'You shall go with the others without me!' interrupted the King.

" 'This I am *not* bound to do,' was his answer   I do not intend to serve abroad save with you!'

" 'By God, sir Earl,' shouted King Edward furiously, 'you shall either go or hang!'

" 'By that same oath, sir King,' shouted Norfolk back at him, 'I will neither go *nor* hang!' "

Aymar paused for a moment, and I saw Joanna bury her face in her hands. "Mother of God," she murmured miserably, "how can I go to my father now?"

"But what did the King say then?" urged the Countess of Pembroke. "Go on, my son!"

"I couldn't hear—nobody could," he told her. "Every man in the hall leaped to his feet and began shouting, some for his Grace, some for Hereford and Norfolk. Then the two of them marched out, their heads high, and that was the end of my first Parliament!" Smiling grimly, he looked over at Humphrey. "I hear your father and Norfolk went their separate ways right from the doors of the hall, gathering men under their standards as they went."

Humphrey nodded. "And we hear the King is seizing our goods when and wherever he can."

"But, Humphrey," protested the Countess, her face white, "surely neither your father as Constable nor our Earl Marshal will take arms against the Crown! It would be treason!"

"It will never come to that. When his temper cools, King Edward will see that they have the right on their side."

"When his temper cools," repeated Jo sadly. "But I cannot wait much longer before telling him what I have done." She spread her arms wide in a mute gesture that made her meaning more than clear. "What shall I do now?"

For a moment no one said anything; then Humphrey raised his head and turned to her. 'If I may make a suggestion, my lady, send your children to their grandfather, wait a few days, then follow them. We all know how deeply he loves children, and yours are more lovable than most."

On looking back I realize how unusual it was for such a young man to offer so sensible a plan or, for that matter, to take any interest in Joanna's problem. But, as I had already observed, Humphrey loved children very much himself and so was better able, perhaps, to imagine how my father might be swayed by them.

In any event, Joanna decided to do as he said and, having learned from Aymar that the Court would now be at Windsor, she dispatched Gilbert, the two little girls, and the greater part of her household there, the rest of us setting out less than a week later.

We tried to be cheerful, but it was useless. Joanna's coming interview with our father hung like a dark shadow over all our heads, and I was aware, as well, that I might never see Humphrey again. I knew that I was a fool for allowing this to make me unhappy, but it did.

As a result, our journey was a quiet one, and, when the round tower of Windsor Castle loomed into sight and we saw the royal pennants fluttering in the April breezes, I told Lady Isabella that I felt like turning and galloping back toward Goodrich.

"So do I," she admitted. "We will both feel the King's anger, Bette, and with good reason. I've spent quite a few restless nights, thinking about it."

It seemed to me that poor Rafe looked ten years older than when we met at Goodrich Castle, and it was apparent from Jo's white face and darkly circled eyes that her nights on the road had been far from restful. Now, as our small cavalcade rode up the approach to Windsor and our trumpeters blew for admittance, I saw Rafe reach over, take his wife's free hand, and raise it to his cheek.

She smiled gallantly at him, turned to smile back at Lady Isabella and me, straightened her shoulders, and, with her dark head high, guided her mount briskly over the drawbridge and into the huge cobbled courtyard.

It was, as usual, filled with people coming and going: nobles, servants, townspeople. Horses clattered their hooves and neighed; dogs barked; voices shouted, rumbled, chattered. All was confusion. Only a few curious eyes bothered to follow us as we made our slow way through the crowd to the huge door. Here we reined in our mounts and waited while Joanna sent a servant to ask for an immediate audience with our father. We had decided on this earlier: that she and I would go to him in our traveling robes, if possible, leaving Rafe to await the result of our interview.

I think I was hoping to hear he was out hunting. I know that when his usher bade us welcome, saying that the King would see us in his privy chamber, my hands trembled so that I could hardly hold the reins and my legs, as I dismounted, almost bent under me.

We walked in silence, climbing the familiar stairs, crossing the antechambers, passing the guards, and entering the room where our father sat on his chair of state. His face was stony and he made no move to meet us or greet us. Instead, he remained motionless and said nothing, watching us approach then kneel at his feet.

He paid little attention to me. His eyes, fixed on Joanna's swollen body, widened in what seemed to be pain and angry horror, and Jo, meeting them, began to shake.

"So," he said at last, heavily, grimly. "The tales I refused to believe about you are true. A daughter of England has proven herself no better than a whore."

"No, no, my lord!" protested Joanna, putting up a hand as if to ward off a blow. "I am wed to Sir Ralph de Monthermer."

At that he stiffened, his face darkening. "When?"

"Late January," she replied in a voice that was all but inaudible.

"And the child will be born?"

"I believe—early in August."

"I see. Do you think that by wedding the lowborn father

of your bastard you have made matters right? That I will call a squire my son and his spawn my grandchild?"

It was now obvious to me that my father's temper was out of his control. I took a tentative step toward him, then fell back as he glared at me.

"And you, Elizabeth, after your own defiance, are here to plead your sister's cause? A splendid pair of daughters for the King of England to bear: What, in the name of God, have I done to deserve this? Have I not been a loving and indulgent father to you both?"

Rising, he pointed to the door behind us. "Go, Joanna, and hide your shame some place out of my sight. From this moment you are no child of mine! I shall not countenance your sinful behavior by allowing you to enjoy the riches and honors heaped on you by your late lord, and your innocent children must remain under my care and protection. Nor will I forgive or recognize your marriage. Where is this—servant?"

At that Joanna's head went back and she faced him directly, her dark eyes flashing. "My lord husband," she announced in ringing tones, "is here with me. As he should be. For no matter what you say or do, Sire, he *is* my husband and we will remain together, for better or for worse!"

"A fine speech, Joanna, but you forget that a daughter of England cannot wed without the King's permission." He clapped his hands and a servant entered. "Summon the Captain of the Guard."

When the man hurried away I forced myself to speak. "Please, sir, allow Joanna to explain!"

"There is nothing to explain, Elizabeth. Your sister has lowered us all by taking a servant as a lover and, after conceiving his child, by wedding him in secret. If this is not true, I will listen. If it *is* true, there is nothing more to be said."

It was true, of course, and I fell silent. In any case, the entrance of the Captain of the Guard, a moment later, stilled any further protest.

"You will find a member of the Lady Joanna's household here in the castle," our father said to him. "Sir Ralph de Monthermer. Take him under guard to Bristol Castle and place him in strict confinement there. Immediately, if you please. If he or anyone else asks you why, it is by the King's orders!"

Ten

I turned to follow Joanna but my father called me back. "We will not be setting out for Holland in May as I had hoped," he said. "Remain at Court or return to Langley. I will see that you have ample warning of the time of our departure, and in the meantime do not give me any reason to be ashamed of *you!*"

Murmuring something, I backed out of his presence and hurried after Joanna, finding her at last just inside the doorway that led out into the courtyard.

"They've taken Rafe away already," she told me. "What am I to do, Bette? What am I to do?" Her voice broke and she swallowed a sob. "Where am I to go?"

Putting my arms around her drooping shoulders, I led her back into a small empty chamber.

"I must stay at Court or return to Langley," I told her. "But he said nothing more about you. I should think you free to go where you please, as long as you remain in seclusion. Why not come with me to Langley?"

She shook her head. "That would not be 'keeping out of his sight.' He visits Langley too often."

I had to admit this was true, but we agreed, too, that although it would be unwise for them to meet again until his anger had cooled, she should be within easy distance of Langley and London so that I could send her word of any change in his attitude without wasting time. Time, now, was of such frightening importance to her and her unborn babe.

We had, I remember, decided against several places for varying reasons when I suddenly thought of Berkhamsted, our Cousin Edmund's castle, situated on the banks of the River Bulbourne about six miles away from Langley.

"Cousin Edmund would be happy to have you there, I'm sure," I said.

"And the Lady Margaret?" asked Joanna grimly. "Have you forgotten that she's Gilbert's sister?"

"She's confined to her bed at Oakham with a broken hip. I would not have suggested Berkhamsted otherwise—although she rarely spent as much as a night there. She hates the place, I believe."

"Well, ask Edmund, Bette. I'm too unhappy to care where I go."

✳

The weeks after Jo set out for Berkhamsted passed swiftly. At first I stayed with my father's Court, thinking it wise to be where I could see for myself any change in his state of mind. His anger toward me soon disappeared, but when I timidly mentioned Joanna one day it flared hotly and he told me sharply not to bring up the subject again.

Everyone else was discussing it, of course, for her marriage was now generally known; and, although nothing was said in the King's presence, our nobles were all taking sides, some arguing that he should forgive her, others insisting that her conduct was indefensible and that such an unsuitable union should be declared null and void. Of these latter critics, a few may well have hoped to win the hand of England's principal and wealthiest countess themselves and were, perhaps, still hoping.

May slipped away, and most of June, and my anxiety grew. A desire for the peace and beauty of the countryside took me to Langley, leaving my father at Westminster, where he was trying to settle his differences with the clergy and his nobles.

It was pleasant to be with my brother Edward, certainly, and I felt my spirits rise even higher when my sister Mary surprised us both by riding up from Amesbury and announcing that she planned to remain with me until I sailed for Holland. Before our mother's death she had been a constant visitor to our royal households, coming and going at will, but in the last few years her duties had increased and I had seen little of her.

We had never been very close, although she was nearer me in age than my other sisters, my childhood having been spent with Edward and she, of course, having taken the veil early in her eighth year. They tell me that I was present at the ceremony, but as I was only four myself I do not remember it.

I do recall being taken to Amesbury by our parents,

both to see her and to see our grandmother, the Dowager Queen Eleanor of Provence, who had retired there after our grandfather, King Henry III, died. Mary, it seemed, was her favorite granddaughter, and she was so eager to have her company in her old age that she gave our father and mother no peace until my sister became one of the nuns of her abbey. It is an ancient order, founded by Queen Guinevere and now a branch of Fontevrault, where many of our ancestors are buried. Mary was supposed to move to France when our grandmother died in 1292 but she did not; if she had there would not be one of us left in England.

I was sitting in the loveliest of our gardens the day Mary arrived, the garden in which our mother planted the grafts of a special apple she brought from Aquitaine many years ago, called the Blanc Durel. Its blossoms had been lavish that spring, but they were gone now, of course, and the fruit still small, and I looked at the little green apples and sighed, thinking that I would never again watch them ripen or see the leaves lose their color and fall to the ground.

How miserable I might have made myself I cannot tell, for Mary chose this moment to join me, her handsome habit trailing along behind her as she bounced briskly down the path. She has always been the most lighthearted of all my sisters and, unlike the rest of us, quite plump. She has, as well, the merriest laugh, and is, in fact, so different from what one imagines a *religeuse* to be that I often forget she is a nun.

She was her usual cheerful self while we embraced and

as she told me that she planned to stay with me for the rest of my time at home; but after I had told her how happy this made me, she turned suddenly serious and, in a voice full of concern, asked about Joanna.

I related the whole story, beginning with the rumors that reached my father before my wedding and ending with his refusal to recognize her secret marriage to Rafe.

"If we could somehow change his mind before the babe is born, Mary," I added, "I would set out for Holland with an easier mind."

She nodded and was silent for a moment or two. "Anthony Bek!" she said abruptly. "He has helped me more than once, Bette, and is the most understanding of all our bishops. Our father respects his opinion, I know, and listens to him. I think he might well forgive Joanna if his Grace advises it."

I agreed instantly, wondering why I had not thought of him myself. The Bishop of Durham was certainly the most influential member of our clergy and, I assured Mary, would be an excellent mediator, the very best.

"Come," I suggested, "Let us write him today."

Soon after our messenger was on his way to his Grace at Westminster, my sister and I decided to join our father's Court there ourselves. The Bishop might want to discuss Joanna's situation with us, we thought; or, as Mary said, a word from her at the right time might sway our father a little—"If there *is* a right time!"

Our sire greeted us warmly, but one look at his face warned us that we must not mention Joanna. He was still at odds with the nobles and clergy, we learned, and faced a whole wasted summer—the summer he had planned to spend fighting the French.

"I have just about made up my mind that you and I will set out in August," he told me grimly, "with or without the aid I have been seeking all these months. So prepare yourself, my daughter, and your people."

As most of my possessions had been readied back in January, I had nothing to do now but wait. A note from Bishop Bek saying he would do his best for Joanna cheered us at first on her account; then, when day followed day without further word, even that hope began to fade.

"We might just as well have stayed at Langley," I said to Mary one afternoon as we sat with our needlework. "We've been here at Westminster for two whole weeks and accomplished nothing."

Mary agreed. "It's so hot here, and the Thames smells so foul," she added. "Shall we ride back there, Bette?"

Before I could reply, Lady Isabella de Vescy hurried into the chamber.

"Hundreds of people are pouring into the courtyard outside the Great Hall," she told us excitedly. "The King is expected to make some proclamation there shortly, and I hear that the Lord Edward came in from Langley an hour or so ago."

Dropping our canvases and our skeins of silk, we followed her to a gallery that overlooked the entrance to the hall. She was right: my lord father had already emerged and was standing on the steps with my brother beside him, facing a group of our noblemen and bishops, all garbed in their most sumptuous robes. In the open space below them was a surging mass of townspeople, pushing, cheering, and chattering.

My father turned to the noisy crowd and raised his arm for silence. Instantly, all was still.

"For your sakes," he said in a voice that even reached us, high up in our gallery, "I am going to meet danger. If I return, receive me as you have been wont to do and I will give you back all I have taken from you."

Then he drew Edward forward.

"If I die, here is my son. Take him as your King!"

A great roar went up from the courtyard, and a forest of arms waved assent. I saw more than one of the nobles and clergymen wiping their eyes, and Edward later told me that the Archbishop of Winchelsea, the leading trouble-maker, broke into loud sobs.

My own eyes were wet, certainly, and when the stirring scene ended Mary and I returned to our privy chamber, assuming that our father had finally gained all that he wished.

But Anthony Bek, who joined us there a little later, shook his head dubiously. "The Earls of Hereford and Norfolk have not yet mended their quarrel with his Grace," he told us, "and the barons and clergy continue to debate acrimoniously behind his back. Well, we shall see, we shall see! In the meantime, my dear daughters, I have good news for *you*. The King has at last agreed to another meeting with the Lady Joanna and has promised me to open both his heart and his mind to her story. The Court moves to St. Albans tomorrow. Bring your sister there, and I will take her to King Edward myself."

✶

By suppertime the next day Mary and I sighted Berk-hamsted Castle: first the round keep, then the curtain walls, interrupted at intervals by ten half-round towers. We approached it from the south, our road leading us directly to the main entrance, and we were soon clopping over the wooden bridge that spanned the outer ditch, then through the great gateway and over the second bridge that crossed the moat. The keep now loomed ahead, standing on a motte some forty or fifty feet high; the buildings in which we expected to find Joanna were to our left on the west side of the inner bailey.

Here we dismounted and were led through the Painted Chamber to the Queen's Chamber, where we fell into Joanna's arms, held out eagerly to welcome us.

"Bette—and Mary!" she said. "I have been *longing* for company!"

After giving Mary a second kiss, she looked at both our faces. "You bring me good news," she announced. "I'm sure you do!"

"Yes, we do," I replied. "But as it was Mary who is responsible, she should be the one to tell you."

$*$

We three left Berkhamsted early the following morning, but as Joanna was so near her time she had to make the journey to St. Albans by horse litter. So, although we had only about fifteen miles to travel, it was midday before we reached our destination.

Without wasting a moment we sought out the Bishop of Durham there. He greeted us so cheerfully that my hopes for Joanna's success began to rise.

"His Grace awaits you," he said, with a smile. "And I am to be present, having intervened for you."

Mary and I followed them into our father's presence. As before, he was seated on his chair of state, but it seemed to me that this time he watched Joanna walk toward him with compassion on his face instead of the cold anger that had so frightened me before.

I thought, too, that Joanna's manner was just as it should be, neither arrogant nor humble, and that her words were well chosen. In a quiet voice she described her unhappiness with Gilbert de Clare and how, after his death, she had grown to love Ralph de Monthermer—and why. Her weary face lit up as she praised her young husband's conduct, and it glowed as she told of his devotion and the happiness they had found together.

Our father did not once interrupt her. Soon after she began to speak, he motioned to a page to bring her a stool, waving her down on it; but he said nothing.

"It is not considered ignominious or disgraceful for a great earl to take a poor woman as his wife," she reminded him, apparently knowing of such a case. "So I cannot see why it is blameworthy or too difficult to promote to honor so gallant a man as my husband."

She rose from the stool with clumsy heaviness, reached for his hand, and lifted it to her cheek. He looked down on her dark, bowed head and I saw his eyes fill with tears. A moment later our father was on his feet, too, and Joanna was in his arms.

Anthony Bek touched my arm and Mary's, nodded toward the door, and, with complete disregard for all the royal rules and customs, we three tiptoed away, leaving father and daughter alone together.

*

It was a transformed Joanna who joined us later in the apartments set aside for the royal family. Her eyes were radiant, she seemed to carry her great belly almost triumphantly, and there was a warm note in her voice as she told Mary and me that all was well between herself and our father.

"I go to Eltham Palace to await the birth of my babe," she said. "Rafe will be released and come to me there! My wealth and honors shall be returned to me, and all I must do is send a hundred men-at-arms with my lord father when he goes to fight the French. He stipulates that Rafe must *not* be their captain"—she laughed as she told us this—"an easy thing to promise, believe me!"

Then, taking a deep breath, she exhaled it slowly.

"Oh, God, I am so happy! I can't be awake—this must be a dream!"

Eleven

$\mathcal{I}$t was the twenty-third day of the month of August before my father and I finally set sail, and, although my heart was filled with sadness for my own lot, I had no more concerns for Joanna; our father never did things by halves, and his recognition of her marriage was all that she or anyone else could have asked.

Rafe, I am happy to say, was released immediately and hastened to his wife. On the second day of August he and Jo did homage to the King and our brother at beautiful Eltham Palace, and, this being done, Rafe became (in Joanna's right) the Earl of Gloucester and Hertford. The united couple then retired to their castle at Marlborough to await the imminent birth of their child.

Perhaps because I was so occupied in preparations for my departure, I find that I have forgotten the date on which the babe was born. I do remember that I was with my father and Edward when Joanna's servant arrived to tell us that she was safely delivered of a girl, already named Mary, and I further recall that they gave the man substantial sums for carrying the news to us.

My last anxiety for Joanna having been laid at rest, I said farewell to my friends and my brother without seeing her again. She, of course, was not yet strong enough to travel, and I was too busy to ride the fifty miles to Marlborough and back again.

Every hour, it seemed to me, was filled with visits from jewelers, silversmiths, artisans who were making my newest chariot and baggage carts, sewing women now working day and night, finishing fresh robes to replace those worn since my wedding, and my own people, whose task it was to pack my plate, linen, kitchen and dining utensils, chapel furniture—all the hundreds of items that must go with me to my new home.

Of all my ladies, Lady Isabella de Vescy was by far the most helpful, having made the same journey with Meg. In fact, she worked so hard over our preparations that I was, for her sake, almost glad when we were finally at sea. As we were a great fleet of more than 350 vessels carrying 1,800 knights and more foot soldiers than I can remember, our sailing was an event of magnitude; many masses were celebrated to ensure a safe voyage, and, for the same reason, we fed 140 of the poor.

I think that my father, too, must have been relieved to see the shores of Winchelsea fade into the distance, for both before and after he boarded our ship, the cog *Ed-*

ward, messengers rode back and forth, to and from London, with letters and documents that kept his brow furrowed and his smile absent.

He became more himself during our slow voyage—Meg reached Brabant in four days, but it was eleven before we finally landed at Sluis and then moved up to Aardenburg, where fresh trouble errupted. Our fleet had been procured mostly from the Cinque Ports and the Yarmouth area, two groups of seafaring men who had been rivals for years. Once the ships were anchored and the crews on shore, they began brawling in the streets. This led to really serious fighting, and before it was over two hundred men were slain and thirty-two of our ships burned.

Shortly before this disaster occurred, however, our entourage set out for Bruges, and we learned of it from couriers who caught up with us along the way. Except for sending back orders to inquire into the matter and punish the offenders, there was little my father could do; and by the time we neared our destination he had put the problem out of his mind and was ready to face what lay ahead.

My own spirits were low, as they had been from the hour we first put foot on foreign soil, but they began to rise when we entered Bruges and proceeded slowly toward its castle.

I was so charmed by its narrow tree-shaded waterways, crossed by the little stone bridges that gave the city its name, that I began to think I might not be so unhappy in my future life. Flanders and Holland were neighbors— perhaps The Hague would be like Bruges.

I must have been smiling to myself, for my father, riding close beside me, asked me what I was thinking about. When I told him he nodded approvingly.

"How you fare lies in your own hands, Bette," he told me. "You can make yourself miserable by repining or you can try to find some happiness in your marriage. You and Jan have a long lifetime ahead of you—God willing! Help him to overcome his fears and shyness, be good friends if you cannot be lovers, and your years together may well be reasonably content."

"I *am* going to try, dear Sire," I assured him. "For I've learned how very much I want children. I go to my lord ready to do what I can to make our marriage fruitful."

"If I may be sure of that, my child, I will say farewell to you with an easier heart "

He was looking at me with such a warm, tender expression on his face that my eyes filled with tears. "I will do my best—that I promise you. And I promise you, as well, that you will never again have cause to say that I am unfit to be a King's daughter!"

Leaning over, he patted my hand. "I'm sure of it. In fact, I expect to be very proud of you—my beautiful youngest daughter, the Countess of Holland."

After that we rode along in silence. Then I spoke, asking a question that had been on my lips for some time "But I need not leave you immediately, dearest Sire?"

"Not immediately, no," he replied, smiling down at me. "I cannot make any plans for you until I know more of my own; certainly I will keep you with me as long as possible."

I could not hope for anything more than this, and his words made the canal beside us doubly lovely to me A lacy willow, hanging over the opposite bank, was a silvery green among the deeper colors of the other trees, and the whole picture was reflected in the unmoving water until a family of swans drifted through it, breaking it up into green ripples.

A great feeling of utter peace filled me, lasting through our arrival at the ducal palace, our meeting with Count Guy—a bald little man with a scruffy beard—and continuing on while we settled into our apartments there. With luck, I told myself, my father would remain in this delightful town for many weeks, and I with him.

How long I enjoyed this dream I am not sure. I know that it was sometime that same evening when my father entered with a hurried step and an anxious face. My ladies rose to leave us alone, but he waved them back.

"No, no," he said. "I must talk to you all. As I think you know, I came here to Bruges to assist Count Guy in fortifying it against the incursions of the French. Now he tells me that the townspeople do not favor our alliance! They dislike him heartily, apparently, and they are seriously considering surrendering the city to the enemy. In the circumstances it is not safe for us here; the French, he says, hope to take us prisoner."

A frightened murmur ran around our little circle, interrupting him for a moment. Then he continued, I thought with a touch of impatience.

"Because of this danger we must set out secretly for Ghent shortly after dawn, taking the lengthy and devious route by way of Antwerp, Louvain, Malines, and Brussels. It is three times the distance, but we dare not travel the direct road or disclose our identity. So wear your plainest robes, no jewels, prepare yourselves for long hours in the saddle, and tell your tiring women to hold their tongues. Only those we know we can trust will be aware of our departure."

Without another word he strode out, leaving us speech-less. Then Lady Isabella turned to me. "Everything must be packed again and we should get what rest we can. If we keep our women right here with us all night, they will not have any opportunity to talk to the other servants." Rising, she moved to the door and clapped her hands.

*

It was a quiet, sleepy group that slipped through the dim, empty corridors, out of the ducal palace, and across the deserted courtyard early the following morning. A man in the Count's livery unlocked the great door for us, closing it immediately behind us. My father, still without saying anything, led the way across a small bridge and into a narrow street, where we saw a little band of squires and men-at-arms waiting for us with horses and one baggage wagon.

As they helped us into our saddles, I noticed that all the horses' hooves were tied up in heavy cloth, which enabled us to ride over the rough cobbles so silently that I do not believe we wakened anyone in the town. Certainly the doors and windows of all the houses we passed remained closed, and we did not see a single face until we reached the Damme gate in the city walls. There another of the Count's men was on hand to see us safely on our way, and we were soon far enough along the road to halt and un-muffle our horses' hooves.

From the moment we rose that morning until we arrived unharmed in Ghent some five weary days later, our journey was without incident. As we spent our nights at religious houses, no one questioned us; and, although we occasionally joined other bands of travelers, more often we had the roads to ourselves. The weather, fair at first, turned wet, giving the pleasant wooded countryside, rather like Norfolk in places, a dreary aspect, and keeping us so busy watching for potholes that we could not pay much attention to the landscape around us.

I had hoped and expected that we would see Meg at Brussels, but the way in which we were traveling made this impossible. As my father explained it to me, it would not be wise for the King of England to arrive at a foreign court incognito and without his usual entourage. "We are not fugitives," he said, "but we would certainly seem to be."

Actually, we skirted the city, and as we rode on, leaving its walls in the distance, my father comforted me by promising to send for Meg—and Eleanora, too—soon after we were established in Ghent.

I shall never forget my first sight of the Count of Flanders' castle at Ghent. I knew instantly why we had come to it: anyone, even the King of England, must feel safe in this huge stone edifice! Once we had crossed its drawbridge we could surely have nothing to fear; we would, I thought, be as secure within its high walls as if we were home in the Tower of London.

I said as much to Count Guy, who, having ridden directly there from Bruges, was waiting in the great doorway to welcome us.

"That is the main reason why you are here and not at Ypres," he said, nodding. "Our home there is more vulnerable to attack—and is dangerously close to the French border. I would have moved my lady here, long since, had she not been too ill to travel."

After I had said all the courteous things, he conducted me to our large and extremely comfortable apartments and left me there. I did not see him again, for he remained closeted with my father until bedtime and was gone when I rose the next morning.

"Back to his wife," was my sire's reply to my surprised question. "He promised to return to us here almost immediately—but I must confess I find his attitude far from what I expected. He's certainly been seeking my aid ever since the French began harassing him last year. But now that I *am* here he seems in no hurry to begin our campaign against them!"

Seeing that he was both weary and angry I changed the subject, telling him how content I was with our quarters.

"Guy has placed the whole castle at my disposal," he said. "Ypres is where he and his family really live, so this is all ours."

We were pleasantly occupied in settling our possessions into this commodious new home; but when that was done I discovered that we had more to worry us than just Count Guy's attitude, for the people of the town soon made it painfully obvious that they resented our presence. Then, after our soldiers arrived, they became openly hostile. We had, of course, expected this from the "Liliaerts," the friends of the lily of France, but not, no, *not* from the Flemings we had come to help!

Several of our servants had complained to me of this; then, to my great distress, I discovered it for myself. My ladies and I, thinking to visit the town market, set out one day on foot. The first townspeople we passed glared angrily and shook their fists; the second group shouted something obviously insulting; and the third, a rough-looking band of young men, advanced toward us in such a menacing fashion that we turned and ran back to the castle gate.

Our royal usher was waiting for us there, his face anxious.

"His Grace sent word that no one should venture into town," he told us, leading us across the courtyard. "But you had already left the castle."

Before I could ask him why, my father, followed by several of our earls who had recently joined us, strode toward me.

"Where have you been, Elizabeth?" He sounded quite angry. "Why did you disobey my order to remain here in the castle?"

"No, no, your Grace," protested his usher hurriedly. "The ladies had passed the gates before your command reached me. I was about to send some men-at-arms after them when I saw them returning."

"We came back because the townspeople frightened us," I told my father. "Why do they hate us, Sire? In any case, I see that you had good reason to keep us within the walls today."

"Very good reason indeed," he replied, "as they may have for their resentment of *us*. I was informed this morning that our soldiers plundered several Flemish towns on their way here to Ghent, after killing two hundred men at Damme who had the courage to resist them. I'm going to the encampment now to find out whether this serious accusation has any truth in it."

"Oh, surely not! I cannot believe our men would do such a dreadful thing!"

"Unfortunately, Bette, I can. You know little of the ways of an army on the march. I do, alas; if this is not just a false rumor I will have the difficult task of punishing the offenders in a manner that will not only prevent a recurrence but will also prove to the Gantoise that I am as horrified by the foul deed as they are."

His voice, I noticed, had the metallic ring I always heard in it when he was most disturbed, his left eyelid drooped, and the lines from his nose to the corners of his mouth were more deeply chiseled than I had ever before seen them.

"After your own experience," he said, "and because of what I have just told you, I am sure I need not repeat my command to remain within the castle walls."

I hastened to agree and stepped aside. My ladies, of course, had heard every grim word, and after we watched the royal party mount their horses and ride away we returned to our apartments in silence. I had no desire, certainly, to discuss the shameful incident; for Englishmen to behave thus was something I would not yet face. There must be a mistake, I told myself, there *must* be!

Some hours later I was still trying to put the matter out of my mind, but an afternoon with nothing to do but needlework is not conducive to forgetfulness. Young as I was, I could understand the wretched position in which we were placed. No wonder my father had looked ten years older than he should!

Everything seemed to have gone wrong for him from the very beginning: the obstacles placed in his way by the clergy and nobles, our difficult journey, the discovery that the people of Bruges wished to surrender to the French and that many here at Ghent were feeling the same—

We had had to flee from Bruges in fear of our lives; here we could not walk the streets without meeting hostility. Why had we come? Why had our soldiers been allowed to kill the people we had traveled so far to help?

Lady Isabella must have been thinking the same disturbing thoughts, for she sighed heavily from time to time and said little. Neither of us seemed to be making much progress with our needles—my silk snarled constantly, I remember—and she surprised me by suddenly throwing her canvas down on a table with an air of complete exasperation.

"With your permission, my lady," she said, rising, "I will leave you for a while. I feel the need of some air."

"Unless you wish to be alone," I answered, "I will come with you. Where shall we walk? Not the courtyard—"

"If you don't mind the stairs," suggested one of our ladies, "You might try the ramparts. I've walked around them every fair day."

It ended with all of us climbing to the crenelated parapet that topped the castle walls and strolling two by two in the crisp late-October air. The views through the apertures were not as extensive as those from most castle ramparts, of course, as this one was not built on a hill or, indeed, on any kind of rise. But the walls were so high that we could see the River Lys, the moat, and most of the town itself spread below us.

The sound of trumpets and marching feet took us to the side overlooking the market square, where we could plainly see that some unusual activity was taking place.

Hundreds of townspeople were crowded into it watching a group of men wearing our royal livery erect a dais with my father's familiar canopy; opposite it, some men-at-arms were tying a heavy rope to the top of a sinister wooden platform.

"It's a gallows!" I said to Lady Isabella in a shrill, shocked voice. "Mother of Mercy, it's a gallows!"

As we stared down in fascinated horror, we saw my father take his place, then stand there while our trumpeters led in a band of soldiers dragging several of their own men. We were too far away to see their faces, but one of the prisoners, when they neared the gallows, slumped down in what must have been a faint.

A loud order rang out, two of the drummers stepped forward and beat a somber roll on their drums, a struggling, shouting soldier was pushed up onto the dread platform, and the noose was fixed around his neck.

I remember gasping and closing my eyes. The drums continued rolling for a moment or two, then stopped. A great cheer rose from the townspeople, and I opened my eyes to see the soldier dangling from the rope, his legs jerking and twitching.

A wave of nausea swept over me and my mouth filled with water. Surely I was not going to vomit here in front of all my ladies! With an effort I controlled the impulse and stepped to the other side of the parapet, taking deep slow breaths of the cool air.

"Come," said Lady Isabella, moving quickly to me and taking my arm. "I have no desire to watch this grim spectacle, God knows, and I doubt very much that the King would want you to. Let the others remain if they wish!"

Twelve

The hanging of our soldiers may have appeased the angry townspeople, but my father still refused to allow us to leave the castle. Because of this, time began to drag painfully for me and my ladies, so painfully, in fact, that I was almost (but not quite!) ready to join my lord in Holland. Our days were drearily alike and there was little to do—pray, ply our needles, walk the battlements, eat our meals.

Our evenings, usually hours filled with entertainment, were spent quietly in our own apartments, for my father and the other nobles more and more often supped with the army at the encampment. When Count Guy arrived every week or so we all joined him, of course, in the hall, but he never remained very long, and I noticed that my father's temper grew shorter with every visit.

What I did not know then was that Count Guy, disturbed and disappointed at the paucity of our army, and, I suppose, by the friction among our men-at-arms, had pointed out to my father that the French forces were much stronger and that it would be futile to move against them at this time. As a result of this they decided to postpone their active campaign and, on October 9, had signed a two-month truce with King Philip.

This was far from what my father had come abroad to do, and I, in my ignorance, made matters worse one day by asking him why he had not sent for my sisters. It was then the end of October, and we had been at Ghent since the ninth day of September; but although Eleanora, at Bar, was some distance away, I could not understand why Meg, only a long day's journey from us, should not ride over from Brussels.

"Because everything is too unsettled," was his reply. "The attitude of the Flemings, my plans. Their presence here would only add to my problems, as I should think, Elizabeth, you would know without my having to tell you!"

"I'm sorry, Sire," I murmured. "It was just that you *said* you would send for them—"

"When I said that, I had no knowledge of the difficulties I am facing at this moment. Nor do I think I must explain my actions or make excuses to my own daughter!"

After that I dared not mention the subject again, and although I kept hoping the strains on his patience would lessen I could not see that they did. Indeed, it seemed to me that they increased, if that were possible, until I was almost afraid to mention *any* subject! That, of course, is an exaggeration, but it is certainly true that he rarely smiled during this period and I began to long for the sound of his deep, heart-warming laugh.

Because his mood was so touchy, I preferred the evenings alone with my ladies; so when we were invited to sup in the hall one night with him and some unnamed guests from home, I was not particularly pleased. In fact, I grumbled a bit at the need to change to one of my more elaborate gowns.

Lady Isabella and I descended to the Great Hall, followed by my other ladies. Our royal chamberlain led us in, placing me two seats on the left from my lord father's chair of state, then escorted the others to a smaller table nearby.

I was barely seated before my father and the rest of the nobles who would sit at the high table were ushered in with the usual pomp and ceremony, so I rose again, as did everyone else in the hall, and watched them approach.

Walking with my father, and looking superb in his rich robes—his tunicle glittering with golden fringe and his dalmatic a dazzling mixture of gold and silver, diapered and bordered—was Anthony Bek, the Bishop of Durham. Before I was over this pleasing surprise, my eyes went to the group behind them and my heart almost stood still.

There, flanked by two of our noblemen, was a handsomely garbed young man whom I knew only too well. It was Humphrey de Bohun, of course, but what he was doing here in Ghent was more than I could figure out in the short time that elapsed before he was brought to the chair between me and the King.

We greeted each other formally; but our eyes, meeting

during the hubbub of everyone being seated, told another story. I'm afraid my face did, too, for I felt myself flush and it was with difficulty that I kept my voice from trembling.

I had no opportunity, at first, to question him or, indeed, to talk with him at all; my father, his face intent, kept both Humphrey and Bishop Bek, seated on his right, too busy for either of them to turn to their other partners.

I listened intently, eating little. They were apparently continuing a discussion begun in the council chamber immediately after their arrival, but I gathered from what they were saying that they were here on a very important mission and that my father was deeply disturbed. I also learned that the Scots had risen again, cutting our forces to pieces at a battle near Stirling, and had then starved Stirling Castle into submission.

"But, Mother of God!" I heard my father say. "Warenne had more than enough men. How could such a disaster happen?"

"If you want the truth, Sire," replied Anthony Bek dryly, "your Treasurer, de Cressingham, dismissed Percy's men for reasons of economy; then, after oversleeping on the crucial morning, Earl Warenne delayed attacking the rebels until he had dubbed a large number of knights."

My father groaned. "Warenne is too old. I should not have left him in charge of our northern forces. The blame is mine, I'm afraid."

"However that may be, Sire," said the Bishop, "this shocking defeat brought everyone to the Parliament in London determined to confirm the Magna Carta and Forest Charter and to clarify just what levies may be made and for what purposes. And that, as we have already told you, was accomplished."

Humphrey had taken part in the earlier conversation, but now my father turned to Anthony Bek and spoke entirely to him, and in a voice so low that I could not hear what he was saying. This brought Humphrey's head around to me, and I asked him why he had come.

"My father was one of the nobles most responsible for pressing the Lord Edward to sign the charters with the new provisions, so he sent me as his own envoy. We have them here for the King to confirm, and I am ready to take my father's part in any discussions that may arise. One of the articles, you see, states that he and Norfolk and their adherents must not be penalized for refusing to serve in Gascony."

"You say my brother signed these documents?"

"As Regent. But Parliament wants King Edward's signature, too."

Before I could say anything else my father reclaimed his attention, keeping it until supper was over. Then, when the tables were cleared away for the dancing, the Master of the Dance brought him to me as a partner.

My mind went back to our first dance together at Ipswich, and as I heard the music begin for the Danse au Chapelet it was all I could do to make my feet behave. We went through the figures stiffly, saying nothing. I suppose we were both waiting for the final one when he must kiss me, remembering the moment when our lips met before.

It came at last, but this time he bent his head awkwardly and merely touched my cheek with his mouth. As he straightened up I looked into his eyes.

"Don't, Bette! Please don't!" he whispered. "I should not have come! Oh, God—this is agony!"

"But you did," I whispered back. "You did!"

"Because I thought you in Holland long since." Glancing swiftly around the hall, he danced the final step ot two, then began to lead me from the floor. "Be careful, Bette," he murmured. "Your father is watching us."

I did what I could to compose myself. A few minutes later I allowed my eyes to drift over to my father and, as Humphrey had told me, he was certainly watching us—and in a way that made me flush guiltily.

I joined my ladies immediately; where Humphrey went I do not know, for I dared not look over my shoulder when we parted, and I did not see him again that evening.

To my great relief, my father left the hall, too, without seeking me out, and I went to bed determined to behave more discreetly. Apparently even that small moment of intimacy with Humphrey while we were dancing had not escaped his notice; from now on I must be more careful. Humphrey and I must meet as old friends and nothing else.

As it turned out, we did not meet at all. I learned later that as soon as my father agreed to sign the charters Humphrey left the castle, setting out for home on the first ship that sailed from Sluis. It was an indescribably painful interval for me—wanting to see Humphrey, to be with him, and knowing that if I did it could lead to nothing but misery.

My father never mentioned him to me, for which I was very grateful. But he did summon me to his privy chamber, the morning after that banquet, to show me the documents he was asked to sign.

"Look well at these pieces of parchment," he said,

handing them to me, "and always remember this moment. When your great-grandfather, King John, signed the Magna Carta in 1215, many ancient wrongs against the people of England were righted, but it made no provision for the expression of the common will. Nor did it sufficiently limit the power of the throne to levy taxes."

He paused, while I scanned the spidery writing, understanding little of it.

"When I affix my name, Elizabeth, as I have decided I must, England cannot be lawfully taxed without the common consent of the realm. And that means, my daughter, that any taxation must be agreed upon by the estates of the realm assembled in Parliament. So by confirming these charters, and the new clauses, I will surrender what has always been a royal privilege—not because I wish to, but because in my heart I know it is right."

Again he was silent, looking intently at me. "If you wonder why I am telling you this, it is because you and I are not free to do what we wish in this life."

✳

The weather turned ugly, as it does in November, and we were now quite willing to remain within the castle walls. The Great Hall and our private apartments had seemed dank and uninviting when the sun was shining, but howling winds in the towers and rain beating against the walls and windows caused the servants to pile so much wood on the fires that the rooms grew comparatively warm and welcoming.

My father, too, appeared more content, perhaps for the same reason. The weeks of fair weather had been weeks of frustration; every clear day that slipped by seemed a day wasted. Now time did not matter—no one but a fool would begin a campaign with the roads deep in mud and winter just around the corner. Realizing this he had, on the twenty-third of November, extended his truce with France until Lent of 1298.

His household, sensing the change in his demeanor, did everything possible to keep him amused. We all supped together again and had music every night. Even without guests we often danced afterwards, and on more than one occasion my dear sire led me onto the floor himself, delighting us with his nimbleness and grace.

Having just finished a lively measure one evening, we were about to return to the dais when we stopped, hearing a bustle at the far end of the hall. It was an usher clearing an aisle through the rest of the company with his white staff, making way for a tall, hooded figure.

It was obviously a woman, but it was not until she reached us, threw back her hood, and knelt before our father that I recognized her. The usher announced, "The Countess of Bar, my lord King!" in his usual ringing tones, but she was already in his embrace.

When she raised her head for his welcoming kiss I saw that she was weeping, weeping so violently that her first words to him were almost unintelligible.

"Forgive me, Sire, for coming to you uninvited, but I need your help! The French Queen has captured my lord!"

Although I doubt that anyone else in the hall heard her, I'm sure they could all tell that something was very wrong indeed. Our father, after stifling an oath, turned to me.

"Take your sister to your privy chamber, Elizabeth," he said. "I will join you there."

After exchanging an embrace, Eleanora and I hurried out of the almost silent hall; as she was still weeping I did not ask her any questions or allow her to talk. When we reached my chamber I untied her cloak, handing it to a tiring woman. To my consternation, I saw that she would soon bear another child and that she looked very, very ill.

Taking her icy fingers in mine I led her to a cushioned seat by the fire. "There!" I said firmly. "A glass of wine, Eleanora, and you will feel more yourself. Now don't say a single word until you are warm and comfortable."

While I poured out the wine and carried it to her she gave me a grateful smile and held out her trembling hands to the blaze. She had regained her composure by the time she took the first sip, and before she had finished it there was actually a little color in her thin cheeks.

Just as she swallowed the last drop our father entered, alone. When she attempted to rise he waved her back, settling himself on a seat by her side.

"Bette has taken good care of you, I see," he said. "Well, my daughter, glad as I am to see you, I could wish that you had sent a messenger to me with your distressing news instead of making so long a journey in such miserable weather and"—he paused and glanced at her swollen body—"in your present state of health."

"I *had* to come, Sire," Eleanora answered. "I felt I could not remain in Bar, knowing that my courier might well be caught on his way to you or perhaps on his return to me with your reply. I would have gone mad, waiting and wondering—" A spasm of coughing shook her, and she was unable to go on.

Reaching over, he took her hand in his. "There, there, child, there there! You are here—and I am happy to have you with us. Now tell me of Henry's capture; tell me everything you can."

Part of her story I knew. My father had given Eleanora's husband a vast sum to use harrying the French; with it he had raised an army of a thousand knights and countless foot soldiers. His first move was to make forays into Champagne, Bar's neighbor, but Queen Jeanne of France, the Countess of Champagne in her own right, had retaliated so fiercely that Duke Henry was soon forced to retreat and employ his men in defending Bar itself.

"But I wrote to the King of the Romans over a year ago," my father told her, "beseeching him as my friend to aid your lord. Did he fail to do so?"

"We heard nothing from him—then or during this last frightening summer. And it was really frightening, Sire! I cannot tell you how dreadful it was for us, never knowing where Queen Jeanne would next strike, where best to mass our soldiers. Then, when she threatened Commercy, Henry found himself caught with an insufficient force to defend it. A battle took place near the city, and he was one of those captured."

Another burst of coughing overpowered her, and our father, rising to his feet, paced up and down until it stopped.

"I blame myself for this," he said sadly. "But the proximity of Champagne was so tempting! And Henry was quite willing to help me, Eleanora, as you know. More than willing, for which I was extremely grateful—extremely grateful."

"He was both proud and happy to serve you, dear lord; and, because he did so, Queen Jeanne loaded him with chains and threw him into a dungeon in Paris, where he may be dying at this moment. If he isn't dead!" The tears that she had been holding back overpowered her again, and she buried her face in her hands.

I went to her and took her in my arms, trying to quiet and comfort her, whispering that she must control herself for the good of her unborn babe.

When her sobs lessened I raised my head and saw that our father was standing staring out of a window, his hands clasped behind his back. He swung around and faced us finally, looking very stern.

"I will do everything in my power, Eleanora, both to free poor Henry and to protect Bar from further attacks. But I can, alas, promise you nothing. All I can do, my dear child, is my very best!"

Thirteen

We put Eleanora to bed and insisted that she remain there. As she sank back on the pillows with a weary sigh, it was shocking to see how sunken her dark blue eyes had become and how lifeless her red-gold Plantagenet hair. It is true that I had not seen her for four years, but I remembered her radiant beauty as a bride, a beauty that was partly due, of course, to her happiness. Then she was thirty years of age and looked twenty; today she was thirty-four and looked fifty.

She seemed a little better the following morning, but I urged her not to rise, bringing my needlework to her bedside and promising to stay there with her. There was much to talk about, certainly. For one thing, she had heard nothing of Joanna's marriage and was much shaken by my long story.

I told her, too, of the quarrels our father had been having with the clergy and our nobles, and all the problems
that had arisen for him here since our delayed arrival; and
when she shook her head and deplored the fact that she
had brought him new trouble, I added the tale of my own
marital difficulties, describing how he had thrown my
gemmed circlet in the fire.

"We don't give him much peace, do we?" I said. "And
Meg, I hear, is just as miserable as ever with Jean."

After that I chatted about more impersonal things and
succeeded in making her drowsy enough to have another
few hours of sleep. But later that day she had several more
severe spells of coughing which seemed to undo the good
her rest had done her.

To my great distress she began, the next morning, to
talk of returning to Bar and her children. Thinking this
madness, I summoned our physician and asked him
whether she was strong enough for the journey. He ex-
amined her, his face grave, and told her firmly that she
must not consider setting out so soon.

"You should not, my lady, have made the effort to
come here," he said sternly, "as I am sure you realize.
Having done so, you must pay the penalty for your im-
prudence."

"But my children may be in danger!" Eleanora protested. "I was afraid to bring them with me, although I
was almost as afraid to leave them at Bar. Now that I have
seen my lord father, I feel I *must* hurry home to them."

"I shall speak to the King, my lady, and tell him quite
frankly that you are not strong enough to do so."

He strode out of the room, and within a very few minutes our father entered, unannounced, and joined me at

her bedside. He stared down at Eleanora silently for a moment; then he, too, shook his head.

"Even I can see that you are not well, my child," he said in an anxious voice. "Forget this nonsense about leaving Ghent, and I will do what I can to set your mind at ease. I shall write Philip, asking him to release Henry; and, to protect Bar and the children, I will send a hundred or so of our men-at-arms there immediately. And," he continued, "in case your people need ransom money for your lord, I will also send them fifteen hundred pounds at the same time."

Before she could thank him he smiled over at me.

"I am ready now to redeem my promise to Elizabeth to invite Margaret to join us here for a visit. What do you both say to her—and Jean, of course—coming to us as soon as possible and remaining to celebrate Christmas?"

Our response was enthusiastic, if a bit disjointed.

He said, cheerfully, "We'll agree, then, to forget our various troubles for the next few weeks and make the most of this interval together. Three of my daughters with me again—for me, certainly, this should be a very merry Christmas."

✳

Although my father's arrangements allayed many of Eleanora's fears, it was still not easy for her to stop fretting over Henry. I did all I could to turn her thoughts to other matters, but with so little success that I almost gave a cheer when, a few days later, we heard trumpets at the castle gates and were told that the Duke and Duchess of Brabant were arriving with a large retinue.

I ran from the chamber and made what haste I dared in

climbing down the winding tower staircase, almost tripping on the tail of my gown more than once. By the time I reached the door to the courtyard, Meg had already dismounted and was standing beside her fat husband, chatting with our steward.

That they had brought a large entourage was immediately evident: they were surrounded by ladies and gentlemen; their armed escort, still on their horses, all but filled the large cobbled area; and, through the gate, one baggage wagon after another was rolling in.

Despite the cold I ran out and, after embracing Meg, I greeted Jean, bade their lords and ladies welcome, and led the way into the castle.

"You should not have g-gone out in that thin robe,' scolded Meg, walking beside me ahead of the others. "Your lips are positively b-blue!"

"I was so eager to see you," I explained, "that I didn't wait for a cloak or anything. I was with Eleanora when we heard your trumpets, and—oh, Meg, I'm so *glad* you've come! I can't tell you how much I'm worried about her—she coughs and coughs and has no strength at all."

"Take me to her now," she demanded. "I'll have my ladies settle into our apartments w-without me."

"There are enough of them, certainly," I commented. "I didn't realize, Meg, that you traveled *en prince*."

She shrugged. "That's my lord's way, Bette, not m-mine. I wanted to leave half of them home in Brussels, but he insisted it would not be fitting. Not f-fitting!" She gave a scornful laugh. "One would think *he* was the K-king of England!"

✶

When Meg and I left Eleanora's bedside I saw that she was extremely concerned. It was most unfair, she said, for this disaster to come to a happily married couple; as she added, grimly, neither she nor I would be so deeply disturbed if the French captured one of *our* husbands.

"How *is* life in Brabant?" I asked her. "And Jean—how is his behavior in his own home?"

"Callous, as always. He brought me one of his bastard sons s-soon after I arrived and flaunted him proudly in my face. A delicate reminder that I have not yet b-borne him a child."

I looked at her, aghast. "What did you do?"

"Welcomed the lad and made him a member of my household. He's a fine boy, born before Jean and I were wed. There are others since, but they remain with their m-mothers. As for my l-life, it's dull. I share in little that concerns m-my lord."

Not knowing what to say, I was silent.

"And you, Bette? Does J-Jan join us here for Christmas?"

I shook my head. "He's too busy preparing for my arrival or some such excuse," I said, not wanting to mention that it was really the ill feeling between Holland and Brabant that was keeping him away. "Needless to say I'm glad to have this last holiday alone with my own family."

"You're lucky. I w-wish I could!"

Meg's arrival raised Eleanora's spirits, and, not long after that, a letter arrived from Duke Henry that helped even more. We found her reading it one morning, her face looking years younger.

"He's been taken from that horrible dungeon in Paris and is now at Bourges," she told us. "Still a prisoner, but they treat him more like a guest now. Oh, what a relief! I was sure he was dead!"

"They wouldn't dare kill him," I said.

"Queen Jeanne might; she's cruel, vindictive, and utterly ruthless."

Neither Meg nor I argued the point. Eleanora could well be right. In any case, her husband's situation was improved and the good news would, we hoped, improve her health. She was allowed, now, to leave her bed for some part of the day, but was not yet strong enough to join us in the dining hall.

Our aim was to have her with us at the Christmas banquet, so we guarded her carefully, doing all we could to keep her from fretting or overtiring her frail body. Our father helped by coming to her when he could, but the thing that cheered her the most was a fresh arrival at the castle—our kinswoman and Eleanora's companion of her youth, the Lady Mary of Bretagne, Countess of St. Pol.

Mary was the daughter of our father's sister Beatrice, who died in 1275 when Eleanora was about eleven. From then until she married the Count of St. Pol and returned to Bretagne, Mary lived at our Court, growing up with Eleanora and Joanna, treated by our parents as another daughter.

It was to see my father that she came to Ghent; Mary had no idea that Eleanora was with us, and the two cousins fell into each other's arms.

My father, however, was not quite so pleased. Mary, like Meg and Jean, brought with her a large retinue, and when she announced that she planned to spend Christmas with us I saw his mouth tighten. He made her welcome, of course, but later that day I overheard him discussing the matter with his Master of the Wardrobe, John de Drokeneford, who held the privy purse.

"I wonder how many more guests we will be expected to house and feed for the next few weeks? This must be placing a severe strain on our already scanty resources!"

"Well, Sire, with all our army expenses and the fifteen hundred pounds we sent to Bar, I must tell you that our purse is almost empty. Until more money comes to us from home, we are, indeed, in very dire straits."

"As if I did not have enough worries without this!" my father exploded, throwing up his hands. "Mother of God, John, I confess to you that my patience is running as low as my gold. Confer with Robert the Panneter and do what you can."

Never in my fifteen years as the King's daughter had I given a thought to the royal purse. Even now, after listening to the fragment of conversation, I paid little attention to the matter. How could the King of England ever need money?

I then put the problem out of my mind so thoroughly that I did not connect it with something that puzzled me one night at supper. It was, I believe, the evening before Christmas Eve, when our knights behaved strangely at their table. Instead of the usual hum of contented voices, punctuated by laughter, they seemed to be eating their meal in a grim silence, broken now and then by what sounded like grumbling among themselves. I tried not to notice but my eyes were drawn to their long trestle, intercepting angry stares directed at our dais.

I asked Lady Isabella later if she knew what was wrong.

"Some fancied slight, I imagine," was her unconcerned reply. "It's not our business, whatever it is."

Because this would be our last Christmas together, we all wanted to celebrate it in the English manner. At home, our castle would be beautifully bedecked and elaborate mummings and every sort of suitable entertainment planned, to say nothing of the lavish feasts provided for each of the Twelve Days of Christmas.

Here at Ghent our festivities had to be on a smaller scale. Lackeys scoured the countryside for appropriate greens, but there was not the variety that grew at home, or the quantity. And whereas minstrels, players, musicians, and dancers of all kinds flocked in England to wherever the King was holding his Christmas Court, knowing they would be welcomed and well rewarded, they either did not come to us here or were not admitted.

Also, it seemed to me, on Christmas Eve, that we were not offered the almost bewildering array of meats, fowls, fish, and sweets that were our holiday fare; but if I gave this fact a second thought it was that our Panneter could not obtain the boars, bucks, swans, pheasants, rabbits, lambs, and so on that he had set before us on other Christmases.

We were, on Christmas Day, a large and determinedly merry party. Eleanora was dining with us for the first time, our table on the dais had been enlarged to about twice its length, and I was told that there were double the usual number of tables set up on the floor of the Great Hall.

I remember that we were ushered to our places with as much attention to the royal rules as we would have been at Westminster or the Tower, so I was quite startled, after we were seated, to see that the knights' table was completely empty.

A hush fell over the assembled company as everyone stared at the unfilled benches. I told myself that our knights were planning some special entertainment for us and had dined early; a moment later, however, they appeared at the entrance and began to march in, one by one. Each man was followed by his personal servant carrying a platter of bread and meat which he placed on the table in front of his master.

When the last knight had taken his place at the long trestle, my father broke the silence.

"Will one of you gentlemen come here to the dais, please, and explain this strange procedure?" Although I could see that he was angry, he kept his voice carefully controlled.

While we all watched, fascinated, a knight whose name I have forgotten rose from the bench and approached our table, falling to his knees before my father.

"The Panneter has not been giving us sufficient food, Sire, so we purchased our own."

My father's face darkened, but before he could reply, Robert the Panneter ran from his place by the entrance through which the food was brought from the kitchens and joined the knight at the dais, looking frightened and distraught.

"I have done my very best, Sire, but how can I buy supplies without money? The merchants insist on being paid what we owe them, and although I told the Wardrobe this—I begged, *pleaded* for enough gold to satisfy them— they refused, saying they could not give me what they do not have!"

He waved his arms in the air as he spoke, his voice growing shriller and shriller with every word, until, at the end, he was all but screaming.

My father stared at them both for a minute or two, his eyes flashing fire. "So. Instead of coming to me with the problem, you prefer to shame me in front of our guests. You, my knights, sworn to noble service, willingly rendered, unfailing unselfishness "—he sounded so coldly scornful as he uttered these familiar phrases that I shivered for every knight in the hall—"and, above all, sworn to gentle courtesy! *Gentle courtesy!* Well, gentlemen, if I may still call you such, I do not think your behavior on this Christmas Day has been either gentle or courteous. However, as food is obviously more important to you than your vows, eat your dinner and try not to disgrace your country and your sovereign again."

While the knight rose and backed away, my father turned his attention to Robert, still kneeling. "You, Robert, will forfeit a month's wages; and if you ever allow such a scene to occur again, you will leave my household. Now out of my sight, sirrah, before I lose what appetite is left to me after this shocking episode!"

With his final word he smote the table in front of him so forcefully that the plate and glass even down at our end jumped and rattled. I put out a hand to steady my own goblet and, hearing an odd sigh from Eleanora who sat next to me, I glanced around.

To my dismay I saw that her forehead was beaded with sweat and her face greenish white. "I'm sorry, Bette—I think I'm going to faint."

Her whisper reached Meg, on her other side, but before we could move she had toppled forward in a dead swoon.

I will not attempt to describe the confusion that followed. My poor sister regained her senses almost immediately, thank God, and was helped from her seat and back to her bedchamber, insisting that she had merely been momentarily overcome by the heat in the hall. Later, when Meg and I talked to her alone, she confessed that it was our father's anger that caused her to faint; we said nothing in reply, however, for we were sure, in our hearts, that she had left her bed too soon and was still far from well.

In any case, she was now quite willing to forego the rest of the holiday banquets and remain quietly in her own apartments, resting and partaking of simpler food; and after the disturbing scene we had witnessed, I, myself, would have been happy to do the same. This, of course, was impossible, but although nothing else marred the meals that followed, it was sad to see how unmerry we were from that time on!

When I say that nothing marred our meals, I do not mean that our household was running smoothly. Far from it. Discontent was rife among the servants, now, as well as among the knights; and we heard, too, that there was increasing trouble between the townspeople and our soldiers, so much trouble that we and our ladies were again forbidden to venture into the streets.

Fortunately for us, we had no particular desire to do so. Our cousin Mary proved to be delightful company, and Eleanora's indisposition kept us all at her bedside a good bit of each day, where we were quite content to chat and sew, not caring that January's snow and winds were hurling themselves against the thick stone walls.

Actually I welcomed the storms; with the new truce signed I knew my father must set out for home—with the army—as soon as the bad weather abated, Meg would leave Ghent, and I would then travel on to my new home. Every hour now was precious to me!

Because she could not go to him, our father often came in to see Eleanora, and I can still see his face on the happy day when she was well enough to receive him in her privy chamber, having left her bed that morning for the first time in weeks.

He kissed her warmly, telling us all that our physician was quite cheered by the way her health seemed to be improving.

"He thinks you may soon join us in the dining hall again," he said. "I have been wanting to give a last banquet here at Ghent, and your recovery, my dear child, will be an excellent excuse for it." Bending, he kissed her again. "But we will not hurry you, Eleanora. I promise you that."

He turned and moved toward the door, pausing to look at a handsome gold cup that sat on the top of a large wooden chest.

"I think I remember this. Did I not give it to you?"

Eleanora nodded. "When you and my mother returned from abroad in the spring of 1286. More than ten years ago, Sire. I carry it wherever I go, for it is very, very dear to me."

"Ah, yes. Those were happy days—happy days! I am glad you have it still to remind you of them. Well, continue to grow stronger, my daughter, and that will make these days happier for me!"

Fourteen

As our Christmas banquet had been such a failure, we, the King's daughters, were determined to make the last one at Ghent all it should have been. A day was chosen when our physician was sure it would not harm Eleanora to attend and, that settled, we sent for Robert the Panneter and contributed gold from our own private purses, thus ascertaining that the food would be varied and lavish. The musicians, at our suggestion, practiced our father's favorite songs and dances; and we, wanting to look our best for him, chose our most beautiful robes for the occasion, bedecking ourselves with ornaments he had given us.

Mine, of course, was the one I wore at my wedding,

with its silver undertunic and surtunic embroidered with silken thread and trimmed with rows of silver gilt buttons. I girdled it, I remember, with a pearl zone that did not arrive from the goldsmith in time for the ceremony, and placed on my head the gemmed coronal that my father threw in the fire, the missing stones having been replaced before we left England.

My women placed my ermine-banded and lined wedding mantle over my shoulders, I glanced in the mirror to make sure nothing was awry, and set out for Eleanora's apartments, thinking her women might need my assistance.

Apparently Meg had had the same idea, for I found her already there, rummaging in Eleanora's jewel casket. "Is this the one you want?" she asked, holding up a gold coronal that flashed with emeralds, sapphires, and rubies and gleamed with dozens of smaller pearls.

"Yes," replied Eleanora, who was sitting down, still only half garbed. "That's it, Meg. It was a gift from France, I think—our father bestowed it on me at the same time that he gave me my gold cup. I shall wear it tonight and a belt of gold and pearls he ordered made for me the year you and Joanna were married. It's in there somewhere."

When Meg rose with the ornaments in her hands, I saw that she, too, was wearing her loveliest jewels. Her crown was heavier than mine, its fourteen foliations studded with unusually large emeralds and huge oriental pearls; an intricately wrought girdle of gold hung low over her hips, and her violet velvet mantle, bordered with sable, was held at the shoulder by a gold clasp in the shape of an eagle.

I was about to comment on her appearance when Eleanora was shaken by one of her attacks of coughing which left her limp and breathless. Both Meg and I asked whether she was quite sure she felt strong enough to endure what must be a wearying evening.

"I shall both endure it and enjoy it," she announced firmly. "Don't fret over me, please. I promise you I shall not faint again!"

Neither of us protested further, and although we watched her with anxious eyes from the time we descended to the hall until, some hours late, we returned with her to her apartments, she played her part magnificently.

So, I am happy to say, did our household, and it was obvious that for our guests—one of them was Count Guy —as well as for us, this evening would never be forgotten.

That our lord father was pleased and proud of his three daugnters seemed obvious, too, and I still remember his well-loved face as he welcomed us to his table, free of strain at last except when he bent to kiss Eleanora. He remained with her on the dais while we danced; then, as the last note died away, he rose to his feet and waved his hand for silence.

"Before bidding you all good night," he said in a voice that reached to the far end of the hall, "I have a pleasant task to perform. Our dear son, Lord Jean, the Duke of Brabant, has not yet received the spurs of knighthood. We cannot observe all the rites, but we can, I think, bestow them on him in the simple manner which is the custom in times of war. Come forward, my lord, if you will."

While Jean, a most unprepossessing figure, moved swiftly and awkwardly to the dais and knelt on one knee, a royal page handed my father his sword and another stood nearby, holding a pair of golden spurs on a fat silken cushion.

The jeweled sword, gleaming in the light of the candles and flares, touched Jean's bent shoulder for a fleeting moment.

"Rise, sir Knight," said the King, smiling warmly down on him.

I glanced at Meg, but it was impossible to guess what she was thinking. This, for a happy man and wife, would be an evening to treasure always. For her the ceremony probably meant little, and when Jean, as was proper, brought her his spurs, she smiled woodenly and avoided his eyes.

Not long after that we retired, accompanying Eleanora to her privy chamber. She was extremely weary, and so were we; the guard at her door drooped noticeably as we approached, and we caught her tiring woman sound asleep by the dying fire.

"Fetch your mistress some w-wine!" Meg ordered sharply. While the woman, rubbing her eyes, hurried to a table and began to fill a small goblet from a tall flagon, Eleanora, who had seated herself on the nearest bench, suddenly straightened up.

"Where is my gold cup?" she said.

The woman looked over at the chest and her eyes widened.

"It was right there, my lady, right there!" In her fright she tipped the goblet, and the wine began to dribble on the floor.

Meg, with an exclamation of disgust, snatched it from her hand and took it to Eleanora. "Drink this! I'll c-call the guard."

But the sleepy man, we soon discovered, was as bewildered as our sister's woman, and our questions led nowhere. He had seen no one either enter or leave the chamber in Eleanora's absence. Yes, he had left his post for a very short interval, but the tiring woman was inside, wasn't she?

Well, there it was. Someone had seen him go, slipped past the snoring woman, and stolen my sister's beloved cup.

"Go to bed," I told her finally. "We'll tell the steward. With luck, the thief is still inside the castle walls."

Although I heard afterwards that every room was searched and every servant closely questioned, the cup was never found. But, as our steward explained to us, many outside people were allowed in the castle on a feast day.

Our father, on being informed of the theft, was even more concerned than Eleanora.

"How many more aggravations and disturbances must we endure?" he fumed. "These weeks at Ghent have been a nightmare! And why did it have to be Eleanora's cup that was stolen? In her feeble health anything of this nature is doubly distressing!"

He glared at the helpless steward, then swung around to face me.

"If there's a similar cup in this city, I shall find it myself and give it to her before we part, Bette. Someone who knows the best goldsmiths must take me to them this very day."

"But your Grace," protested the steward, "I could have every gold cup in Ghent brought to your privy chamber within the hour!"

"And, by doing so, deprive me of an excellent reason to leave these cursed walls for an hour or two. Thank you, but no."

"Please, Sire," I interrupted, "let me go with you. Please —I've been mewed up, too, for what seems like forever. And I think I remember just how the cup was wrought."

The day being clear and the goldsmiths' shops an easy walk from the castle, we presently set out on foot, accompanied by a band of men-at-arms and a member of Count Guy's entourage who had been chosen to be our guide.

There were only a few townspeople in the square as we crossed it, and although most of them paid little attention to us, a group of shabby, noisy boys, followed by a barking dog, trailed after our party until we reached a narrow street and entered a small shop.

They were gone, however, when we emerged without what we were seeking, and we proceeded on to the next one free of any further annoyance. It was, I think, in the fourth place we tried that I saw a footed covered cup enough like Eleanora's to please my father. It stood on a shelf in a dim corner, and when the goldsmith lifted it down and carried it into the light we were both delighted with it.

"Bring it to the castle," said my father, "and you will be paid for it."

Leaving a happy man behind us, we began to retrace our steps. We had not gone far, as I remember, before a man darted from an alley and, with what sounded like an oath, spat on the hem of my father's robe. While our men-at-arms surrounded him and dragged him away, I saw curious faces appear at most of the doors and windows, but no one ventured out until we were almost back in the square. Glancing over my shoulder, then, I noticed several people standing on the cobbles, staring after us.

They no longer looked merely curious; they looked angry, and I moved a little closer to my tall father, feeling almost frightened. He gave me a bleak smile, his left eyelid drooping as it did at such times, and said wryly, "They are not very friendly, are they? I must try to discover what fresh reasons they have for hating us!"

We walked more rapidly now, for the pleasure in being away from the castle was completely ruined. The square was even emptier than before, and I was suddenly struck by the fact that there were no women in the small groups of sullen-faced people who drew aside as we made our way to the castle gates.

We were encircled by our men-at-arms, of course, but when we reached the narrow wooden drawbridge they moved back to make it possible for us to cross it together. I had one foot on it, actually, then withdrew it as a shout went up behind us. A second later an arrow flew past us, missing my father's head by inches and landing in the moat with a small splash.

That was the last I saw of my father that day. I went immediately to my own chamber and summoned Meg there to tell her of his narrow escape from death, deciding, as we discussed it, not to worry Eleanora with the story. He, we heard later, spent the next few hours closeted with Count Guy and our nobles, settling what, if anything, should be done about it.

Having supped quietly with my sisters, I retired early; I was still tired from the preceding night and this fresh incident added to my exhaustion, making it impossible, I soon discovered, to sleep. How long I lay awake I do not know, but every time I closed my eyes I saw that arrow whizzing past my father's head, imagining, as you do in the long nighttime hours, the greater horror that might have occurred.

Meg looked tired the next morning, too, and we agreed that the sooner we all left Ghent the happier we would be.

"I keep urging our f-father to return with us to Brabant," she said. "It is on the w-way home for Eleanora and we can promise you all a w-warm welcome from our people. There, I know, he will be safe!"

"He faces the problem of moving his army back to England," I told her. "When I was with him yesterday, he said the Scots are making trouble again and he must not linger. This is the third day of February. I wonder how soon the seas will be calm enough for them to set sail?"

We were with Eleanora later when our father walked in, carrying the gold cup in his own hands. "Here you are, my daughter," he said, setting it down on a table by her side. "As I suppose Bette told you, she and I found this for you in the town."

"Yes, but she did *not* tell me what I heard from someone else—that you risked your life doing so. If that arrow had found its target, Sire, I would never have forgiven myself."

"It was a bad business," he admitted, his face settling back into the deep lines we now knew so well. "A very bad business indeed! We have reason to believe that my assassination was the signal to massacre all our countrymen here in Ghent and that Count Guy's own sons may well have been involved in the plot. Poor Guy will not believe it, but I'm afraid the rumor is true."

"Then we are all in danger!" I cried.

"Not here in the castle. It is one of the strongest fortresses in Europe, and our army is just outside the town walls. But I have finally made up my mind that we will leave this accursed place the day Eleanora is strong enough to leave with us."

"Today, Sire, today!" she protested vehemently. "Do not linger here one hour on my account. Let us set out for Brussels immediately!"

Meg began to urge him, too, and I was about to add my voice to the chorus when the door opened and the Captain of the Guard rushed in, looking distraught, with Count Guy and Meg's Jean right at his heels.

"Your Grace, your Grace," he began, sounding terrified, "the townspeople are slaying every Englishman they can lay their hands on, and armed bands of Gantoise are approaching the castle gate!"

Neither Count Guy nor Jean said a word. They just stood there waiting for my father to speak.

"Mother of God!" was his instant response. "These are your people, Guy! Go out to them and bring about order, warr them tnat they will be punished—do something!"

"I'm sorry, Sire, but I don't dare. It's too late for that. By standing your friend I have, they say, become their enemy. You just don't understand! All of Ghent has risen against us."

"Then they will discover, by God, what it means to threaten the King of England! Call out our Guard, Captain. Arm every servant in the castle. Set the women to heating lead and water, man the ramparts—" While my father rapped out his commands he strode to the windows that looked over the town, stared down for a moment, then swung around and faced Count Guy again.

"There is obviously no way to summon the army, no

way through that crowd, and they will barricade the city gates—probably have by now. So tell me quickly, my lord Count, which is the safest place in the castle for the ladies?"

"The top of the keep," he replied instantly. "With a few men there, more at the bottom, and two or three on the platform halfway up that has the two doors leading into its own missile storeroom, no one could reach them."

"Thank you." If there was a bitter note in my father's voice, I doubt that Count Guy was aware of it, for the poor man was trembling, as he stood there, and actually wringing his hands. "You heard what the Count said, ladies," continued my father "Gather up what you will need for some hours. It is a cold day: warm cloaks, food —but I need not waste precious time telling you this. Just remember that you are the King's daughters, Eleanora, Margaret, Elizabeth, and take care of the others."

Without another word he hastened out, leaving an appalled silence behind him. Eleanora was the first to come to her senses, issuing a series of orders in a calm manner that did much to quiet my fears and those of not only the other ladies but also two tiring women who happened to be in our chamber at that moment.

I remember little of what occurred next, although I have a very clear recollection of scrambling up the narrow circular staircase with an armful of something. I realized how difficult it would be to mount them with a weapon— thinking of our invaders—and when I reached the top I shared that comforting thought with the others.

The weak February sunshine helped to raise our spirits, and after choosing a sheltered spot, we wrapped Eleanora in a cloak or two. Then we ordered her to remain where she was, no matter what seemed to be going on, and the rest of us began to move back and forth on the parapet, watching first the activity in the inner bailey and then in the town square below.

Both were scenes of utter confusion. The din was unbelievable. In the castle courtyard, everyone seemed to be shouting: men rushed into it from the castle carrying arms: those already there shouted orders to their comrades; dogs barked; women's voices rose above the men's shouts; horses, being hastily arrayed for battle, neighed shrilly.

But the sounds that reached our ears from the town side of the walls were horrifying as well as deafening. There actual fighting was taking place, and we could hear only too clearly the screams of the wounded and dying. From just below us, and from other vantage points on the ramparts, our people were pouring boiling lead and water on the crowds storming the gates. Arrows and missiles, shot or thrown from the loopholes in the thick walls and the embrassures around the battlements, were finding human targets with sickening results.

It was more than I could bear, after a few minutes, and I ran back to Eleanora and crouched by her side, hiding my face in my trembling hands. There we both remained until I heard a new sound.

"Trumpets!" I said to her. "Trumpets, Eleanora. And I hear men marching!" I rose and ran back; she followed me.

We clutched each other and stared down on the city. There, filling the narrow streets and jamming the alleys that led into the square, was a mass of men-at-arms. As they came nearer I was able to recognize a fluttering pennant.

"They're our men, Eleanora!" I think I screamed it to her. "Our soldiers from the encampment! There's a Welsh banner—here come hundreds of our great, brave Welshmen to rescue us!"

Fifteen

I stood on the deck of the ship that was taking me to Holland and watched the sails of my dear father's fleet disappear on their way home to England. Shivering, I clutched my cloak closer around me; it was one of those bleak March days that make you doubt the eventual arrival of spring, turning both the sky and the water a forbidding, grim gray.

If the weather was chill, my heart was cold as ice. Foolish though it seems now, my life, at that moment, appeared to be over. As the white dots faded out of sight I said a final farewell to everything I knew and loved, and, remembering the other farewells I had said in the last few days, I felt slow painful tears begin to run down my cold cheeks. My sisters' faces when we parted in Brussels and my father's as he kissed me for the last time after lifting me into the barge that waited to take me aboard the vessel on which I was standing, all three passed in front of my wet eyes.

Would I ever see them again? Meg, of course, lived not too far away. But Eleanora—so many miles lay between Holland and Bar! And as for my father, my kind, loving, generous father, soon to be across the vast stretches of water—better not think of him until I grew more accustomed to our separation.

I turned and looked back at the shore, but Sluis, the port from which we had sailed, had already faded away. We were moving swiftly now and the air was growing even chiller; the favorable wind for which we had waited several days was blowing steadily, cutting through my fur-lined cloak and making my teeth chatter.

With a heavy sigh I raised a hand, brushed away the last few tears, and joined my ladies in the crowded cabin.

✳

My thoughts during the remainder of the short voyage were mostly with Eleanora, now on her way home to Bar and still in very ill health, and with Meg, living her unhappy life in Brussels, where we had all spent a few uneventful weeks after that frightening day in Ghent. Inevitably, of course, they turned to the future and my own life: would it resemble Meg's or could I, with my determination to make the best of things, find some way of improving the situation between my lord and me?

Meg's home was vast and richly furnished, and so many noblemen poured into it to dine or sup with Duke Jean and my father that our sire was quite struck by the wealth and power of Brabant and complimented his son-in-law on the great number of his liegemen.

But when he spoke to Meg about how comfortably she

was established, she shrugged. "Better a dinner of herbs where love is," she quoted bitterly, "than a s-stalled ox and hatred!"

Her one source of pleasure, she told us later, was in rebuilding an old, almost ruined castle some eight miles or so away near Vilvorde. It was called Veuren and was to be a summer retreat for Meg, surrounded by beautiful gardens and promenades. "You must come and visit me there," she insisted. "At Veuren *I* am the m-mistress—not the cipher I seem to be at B-brussels!"

Would I be a cipher in Holland, I now asked myself? Or would I, like Eleanora, be beloved by my lord's people and share in his rule? Was I too young to hope for this—and was he? Had the year since our marriage brought him more wisdom and perhaps softened the memory of our miserable nights together? Was I now enough of a woman to help him be a man?

All these questions raced through my mind as we neared our destination, and when we were put ashore at Vlaardingen Lady Isabella de Vescy, perhaps sensing my unease, held my hand closely in hers until my young husband, followed by a group of richly garbed lords and ladies, advanced toward me. She dropped it, then, and stepped back, leaving me to meet him alone.

With a pounding heart I braced myself to begin my new life. From this very moment I would, as I had promised myself and my father, do my part—more than my part. So, instead of waiting for Jan to reach me, I ran swiftly to him, my arms outstretched.

"My lord!" I said warmly. "My dear, dear lord! I am so happy, so very, very happy, to be here at last!"

His mouth, slightly agape as always, opened even more, and his eyes widened in astonishment and what might be dismay. I suppose he had been planning to greet me with a formal speech of welcome, carefully composed by someone else and learned with difficulty.

What he did, in the face of my unexpected behavior, was to embrace me feebly, kiss my cheek, and mumble something I could not quite hear.

Fortunately for both of us a dark-visaged man who introduced himself as Wolphard de Borsolen, Lord de Vere, stepped forward immediately and, in a rush of flowery phrases, said all the customary things, making it unnecessary for Jan to take any further part in the little ceremony. I replied as best I could, remembering my father saying that this man had taken Thierry de Brederode's place as Jan's adviser at his own suggestion. My father had then explained why he had chosen Lord de Vere. "I have learned," he told me, "that de Brederode, although a fine man, leans to the French. It is quite the other way with de Vere, because King Philip holds two of his sons prisoner."

It was easy to see that Jan approved of my father's choice; all during the sixteen-mile ride to the Hague, and at the banquet that followed, he kept the tall, dark-haired, swarthy, and (I thought) ugly nobleman constantly at his side, turning to him when there was any question to be settled, deferring to his opinion on every subject that arose, laughing too loudly at his few mild witticisms.

This did not surprise me, of course, for Jan had always been easily led and influenced. As a small boy he had trailed the stronger-minded lads in the royal household with slavish devotion, eager only to be liked and amused. I had hoped, for both our sakes, that he might, by now, be learning to stand a bit more on his own feet; if so, there was no evidence of it that first evening.

We had reached my new home shortly before dark, and I was delighted to find that the royal palace, built by my lord's grandfather, was beautifully situated. A lake called the Vyver lay beside it, a park filled with animals surrounded it, and, I was told, thick woods extended from the edge of the park to Scheveningen, a little village by the sea, less than three miles distant.

I sniffed as we approached the palace gates, and it did seem to me that I could smell salt in the fresh, chill March air, but a moment later we were in the courtyard being welcomed by Jan's household and I was too occupied in returning their greetings to notice anything else.

Once inside the huge dark stone edifice, however, I knew that I would be comfortable here. It was very much like our castles in England, with one spacious chamber opening into another and, as I discovered at supper, with a Great Hall that seemed even larger than the one we had so recently left behind us at Ghent.

My lord sat on one side of me, Wolphard de Borsolen on my other, and the lords and ladies who had traveled with me from home were placed farther down the table among Holland's highest nobles. As a bewildering array of food and wine was offered me, I heard cheerful voices and laughter around us; but Jan, when he spoke at all, sounded so ill at ease that I found it difficult to respond.

I remember swallowing a piece of peacock—to this day I cannot eat it with any relish!—and finding myself on the verge of tears. My good resolutions, my plans to make a life of contentment with my young husband, forgetting Humphrey and thinking only of how best to find happiness with Jan, suddenly seemed to me impossible, a task too great for anyone. And the night ahead of me, which I had promised myself to face with such courage, now loomed like a dark cloud, frightening me so much that my appetite fled and I could barely smile at my other neighbor's pleasantries. I tried to talk and so did Lord de Vere, but before long we were all three sitting in a strained silence, and I was miserably torn between my dread of the midnight hours to come and a weary desire to have this interminable meal end.

When it did I rose, saying, I hope, everything that I should, and retired to my apartments. After my tiring women removed my jeweled coronal, took off the elaborate robe I had chosen for this first evening in my new home, and made me ready for my bed, I dismissed them and settled into it, sitting up against the large soft pillows.

At first, as I waited for Jan to come to me, I was wide awake and taut as a lute string. An hour passed and I no longer heard voices and footsteps in the adjoining chambers; all was so quiet and I had had such a long tiring day that, despite myself, I began to feel very drowsy and had to fight to keep my eyes open.

When I finally fell deeply asleep I do not know, but I awakened to find it morning and the place beside me still empty. As it turned out, the day that followed was such a busy one that I had no time to wonder at Jan's absence nor a moment alone with him when he might have excused himself to me. Many festivities had been arranged for my arrival, and as one ended and another began Wolphard de Borsolen was always with us, his dark eyes watchful, his manner that of an indulgent guardian.

For some reason his constant presence began to irritate me, and I had to remind myself that my father had chosen him to take care of us and that I should be grateful for his

thoughtfulness and attention. Under his firm guidance Jan
and I moved from tiltyard to feast table, from feast table
to dance floor, and from dance floor to our seats under the
canopy on the dais, until I felt like the trained animals
brought in to entertain us and our guests.

Toward the end of the evening I began to think of the
night and some way to tell Jan that I would welcome his
company.

"My apartments are very comfortable," I began a little
hesitantly. "They tell me you chose much of the furnishings yourself. When you come to me I will show you the
beautiful things I brought from England."

It seemed to me that he shied like a frightened horse.
Again, as he had at our meeting, he mumbled something
vague, then began to talk rapidly of the palace itself and
how much his father, Earl Florence, and his mother, the
Countess Beatrice, had loved and improved it.

"The builder is supposed to have known a secret that
made all the beams impervious to filth and rot," he told
me, "and that would even prevent spiders from spinning
their webs there. I find it very hard to believe, I must confess."

"We might refrain from cleaning it for a year or two," I
suggested, "or bring in some spiders and see what happens."

For this mild pleasantry I won a mild smile; then another
awkward silence fell between us, lasting until we rose to
retire.

Not knowing whether to expect him or not, I prepared
for bed and dismissed my ladies and women. I did not,
however, remain awake for long. If he came to me, I
would try to be a dutiful wife; if not, the problem must
be faced later and a sleepless night would not solve it now.

He did not come then, or the next night, or the next. Perhaps, I told myself, he was waiting for the celebrations of my arrival to be over.

But they were, our life settled down into a more quiet pattern, and the other side of my wide bed remained empty. For a little while I felt secretly relieved and began to enjoy the warmer weather and the pleasant countryside. April passed and it was May, and I still shut my eyes to my problem; then a messenger rode in from Bar with a letter that made me forget everything else.

Eleanora was dead. Our dear, gentle sister was gone, her unborn babe with her. And she had died without ever seeing her beloved husband again, for Lord Henry was still imprisoned in France.

Sixteen

On looking back I realize how fortunate we had been for so many years. We had, it is true, lost brothers and sisters in infancy, but from the time that I was old enough to know and love the rest of our large family, not one of us had even been very seriously ill.

But when I first read the news of Eleanora's death I was too overwhelmed by sorrow to be comforted by this fact or, indeed, by anything else. I remember dropping the letter on the floor and running to my bedchamber, where I wept into my pillows for the remainder of that day.

My English ladies, unfortunately, had gone home by now, and although the Hollanders who had taken their places were kind and attentive there was nothing they

167

could do to ease my grief. They tiptoed in and out, bringing me things to eat and drink; they pulled a coverlet over
my shaking body; they shut out the sunlight and, when
I fell into an exhausted sleep, allowed no one to disturb
me.

What I wanted most, of course, was to be with Meg,
and I sought out my lord the following morning to tell
him that I wanted to go to Brussels immediately.

"I'll ask Wolphard," he said.

"I don't see why you should," was my instant response.
"Surely I may visit my sister whenever I wish. What business is it of his?"

Jan shrugged. "He concerns himself in everything we
do. And if you want to know why, my lady, question
your father, not me. He made me promise to be guided in
all things by Wolphard, and I assure you I have no inten-
tion of breaking that promise. I like Wolphard, but unless
I obey him implicitly he can make my life extremely un-
pleasant!"

I looked at him in amazement. "Why, what could Lord
de Vere do to you, Jan? You are the Count of Holland."

"He can lock me up, for one thing. He has."

"But this is dreadful!" I protested. "My father meant
him to be a counselor, a helpful older friend, someone to
advise you! I'll write him, Jan, but in the meantime there
must be other nobles here who will understand your situation and put a stop to this—prevent him from treating you
like a child."

"Well, there aren't. Not any more. Wolphard has ban-
ished from court everyone but his own followers."

"Jan!" I stared at him in disbelief. "If this is true we
must do something about it *now!*" I know I sounded as

disturbed and indignant as I felt; Jan, to my surprise, seemed quite placid and unmoved.

"Why? I tell you, I like him. As long as I don't cross Wolphard we have great times together, and he sees that I have nothing to worry about. He has my seal, he gives orders in my name; I don't even have to read all those long dull documents that I sign."

Too stunned to speak, I sat and looked at his foolish, handsome face, thinking, with horror, of the long years ahead. Young as I was, I knew enough to see what our future might be if this was the way Jan wanted things arranged for him. I had always known that he was weak, but not *this* weak!

Apparently my father had, however, and that was why he had provided him with such a strong guardian. As Jan had just said, Wolphard was my sire's choice. Who was I to question it? And, by the same token, why should I worry? Undoubtedly Lord de Vere knew what was best for us and for Holland.

I rose and Jan rose with me. "I'll speak to Lord de Vere myself," I told him. Then, struck by a sudden thought, I reached over and placed my hand on his. "Come with me to Brussels, Jan. It would please Meg, and I would like to have my husband at my side."

Turning a fiery red, he dropped his eyes from mine and moved his feet uneasily. "Well, perhaps—if Wolphard thinks I should."

Realizing that it was futile to urge him further, I hurried to the room where Lord de Vere was usually to be found. He was seated at a table strewn with documents, so intent that he did not hear me enter. His brow was wrinkled, his thick black eyebrows almost meeting as he studied the paper in his hand, and I decided, watching him, that I had let those black brows prejudice me. If Jan liked him so much he could not be as disagreeable as he seemed.

As soon as we had exchanged greetings I told him of my sister's death and, speaking in my most friendly manner, said how very much I wanted to go to my sister Margaret at Brussels. "And," I added "I have asked my lord to accompany me there."

For a long moment he was silent, his face thoughtful. Then he shook his head. "I'm afraid not, my lady. You go, certainly; I will be happy to arrange for an escort to take you and your ladies to Brabant. But not Jan."

I opened my mouth to protest, then closed it as he spoke again.

"I'm sorry, Lady Elizabeth, to refuse you this—or anything else. The truth, however, is that the lad is still very young, younger than his years. He needs, I have discovered, a strong hand to guide him every hour of the day; we must be patient, you and I, and hope that in time he will be better able to fulfill his duties as Earl of Holland—and as your husband. Until that happy day, I think it wise to keep him under my eye."

✗

There being nothing to delay me, I left The Hague the next day and reached Brussels to find Meg as glad to see me as I was to be with her. We spent the few following weeks together in a seclusion made possible by our mourning for Eleanora, and although I cannot, because of our grief, say it was a happy time, it was peaceful. This was an interlude in which we were relieved of the usual household responsibilities, doing, during the pleasant summer days, only what we wanted to do, seeing only those we wished to see, avoiding by silent agreement any talk of our unhappy marriages.

For me this was quite easy as I heard nothing from Jan or from anyone else in Holland, and, there seeming to be no reason to curtail my visit, I remained with Meg as long as I decently could. Eventually, seeing that it was time for her to resume her normal way of life, I bade her a reluctant, tearful farewell and set out for home.

Home? Could I call it that? To me that word had always meant warmth, love, safety, the place where your heart belongs. There are, I know, wanderers on this earth who have no home; some, although I find this hard to believe, by choice. But everyone else, I am sure, wants, needs, and clings to the dwelling, be it hut, hovel, house, or palace, that is home to him or to her.

The word echoed hollowly in my mind, I remember, as I rode into the courtyard at The Hague, dismounted, and made my way to my own apartments. It was a hot July day and there were very few people around; the steward who greeted me said that my lord and his guardian were in Dort and that much of the household were away from the palace for one reason or another.

The corridors seemed almost deserted and my chambers airless and gloomy. But this *was* my home, and I knew that from now on I must make the best of it and of my equally empty life. My weeks in Brabant had been a respite only; now, here—here in these thick stone walls—I was destined to pass the dull hours, days, weeks, months, and years that lay ahead, a wife in name only, perhaps forever, with few duties and fewer pleasures.

My ladies were kind, of course, and well-meaning, but

there was not one of them to whom I was drawn, for whom I felt any real affection. Wolphard de Borsolen had chosen them, and it is possible, I suppose, that he purposely avoided placing anyone near me who was young and gay, thinking we might make problems for him if he did.

If that is so he succeeded only too well, for I do not recall ever discussing anything of a personal nature with them or sharing any but the mildest of jests. Their faces were much alike—round, placid, smiling; their voices monotonous; their talk uninteresting and predictable.

What we did discuss were the usual topics of polite conversation: the weather, our needlework, the shortcomings of the servants, our future guests, and any change in the length of our sleeves or the draping of our gowns.

Had I been born and raised to this kind of quiet life it would not have been so difficult for me. But this was all so different from my busy years in England, moving from one royal household to another, households seething with activity in which even the youngest of us had some part. Here I had nothing to do but pray, ply my needle, pray, dine, ride when the weather was fair, pray, sup—and pray.

Except for the fact that there were men in our household, I could almost have changed places with my sister Mary and not known any difference!

How my lord amused or occupied himself in the next few months I do not know. I know that he and Lord de Vere spent less and less time at The Hague and that between August and early December I could count on the fingers of my two hands the evenings I passed in their company. I certainly did not care very much, and during the summer and autumn it was easy to find excuses for his constant absence.

But with December came the thought of Christmas and its revels, and my spirits began to rise. I was, after all, still so young that I craved the weeks of merrymaking that Christmas always brought with it, and even without my own family and friends around me I hoped to find enjoyment in the festivities.

I busied myself for a while, making sure my loveliest gowns were ready for the gay evenings to come, thinking that as this would be my first Yuletide in Holland as its Countess I must appear at my very best. Then Lord de Voorne, the husband of Wolphard de Borsolen's daughter, came to stay at the palace with us for a few days, and I learned something so disturbing from him that, for the moment at least, I stopped thinking of the holidays ahead.

He was one of the noblemen who had been there to welcome me to my new home, and I remembered thinking him the most pleasant of them all: not handsome, perhaps, but very likable and extremely easy to talk to. His wife, having just given birth to their first child, had remained in Voorne, which is situated in Zealand, and she did not accompany him this time, either.

I was so grateful for his company that I made the most of it, using his presence as an excuse for a banquet or two and entertainment in the evenings. He had many friends here in The Hague, as I'm sure he had every place he went, and they flocked to the palace to be with him, filling the dreary place with noise and laughter for the first time in many weeks.

But after a while our guests did not laugh so much, it seemed to me. They gathered in small groups, their faces unusually serious, and talked in low voices, falling silent whenever I happened to pass by. I thought little of this the first few times it occurred; you become accustomed to such things when you are a King's daughter. But finally I grew worried—even a bit afraid—wondering just what was wrong.

At home I would have questioned my ladies; they always had some way of discovering what was going on around them. I was reluctant to do this here, partly because I was not used to discussing such matters with them, partly because I doubted that they would tell me anything even if they could. What I decided to do, and did, although it was not easy to arrange, was to talk privately with Lord de Voorne, who was almost always in the center of these anxious-looking groups.

At least we were now on such friendly terms that when we did have a moment alone I was able to speak freely.

"I know there is something wrong," I said to him. "Please tell me what it is, my lord. I grow increasingly concerned."

At first he made no reply, his face thoughtful. Then, as if making a great decision, he sighed, squared his shoulders, and began to speak.

"I don't know what to say to you, my lady. There *is* something very wrong indeed—but whether I should tell you is another matter. *My* situation is extremely difficult and, if I *do* tell you, yours will be, too."

"My situation is already difficult, my lord," I assured him. "Whatever you tell me cannot make it much worse."

"Then, because I need your help—Holland needs your help—I shall take you into my confidence. The truth is that our people are on the verge of revolt. The Lord de Vere— in your lord's name, of course—has been subjecting them to such cruel laws and imposing such exorbitant taxes that the whole country has turned against them. I hear it from everyone—I, his own son-in-law! And I must confess, my lady, that my sympathy is with them, *not* with my wife's father."

I saw what he meant by the difficulty of his situation, and mine, and I told him so. "Lord de Vere was my father's choice," I said, "as, certainly, you know. If what you tell me is true, he has been deceived in the man. What is to be done?"

"Could you not influence your husband to speak for himself? *You* could tell him how wrong, how dangerous, it is to be used in this manner."

I shook my head. "I have no influence of any kind with my lord. We share nothing—nothing. The one time we talked together about Wolphard's influence, he said he liked him. That Wolphard locked him up if he refused to do as he was told, but when all was going smoothly they had great times together. Jan doesn't want to be burdened with Holland's problems, my lord. He doesn't even want to read the papers he signs." Then, seeing the understanding look on Lord de Voorne's face, I went even further. "Jan is a weak, stupid boy. It's not his fault; that's just the way he is."

De Voorne nodded. "I'm afraid you are right, my lady. But you are neither stupid nor weak, if you don't mind my saying so. What I hoped—and many of our nobles have said the same thing to me—was that we might work through you to weaken Wolphard's hold and, later, to rule Holland more fairly. It would not be the first time, my lady, that the wife wore the real crown."

I shall never forget the feeling of warmth that swept over me as I listened to him. After the long months of loneliness, of being unwanted, of thinking my whole life might be wasted, it was as exhilarating as strong wine to know that he and the other noblemen thought me worthy of taking part in Holland's affairs, and my heart sang.

"I will do anything!" I replied, smiling into his eyes. "Just tell me, my lord, and I will do it!"

"First, write your father the King. Tell him what I have told you, and ask for his help in unseating Wolphard. After that, we will see."

Seventeen

That talk with Lord de Voorne made such a difference in my state of mind that I now cared very little about the Christmas revels. As it turned out, it was a good thing I did not, for they were nothing like the gay celebrations to which I was accustomed. In Holland, I learned, the holidays center around the children; it is a family observance, not a time of feasting, mumming, drinking, and dancing.

Jan did return for a few days. In fact, he came to The Hague on Christmas Eve and remained at the palace until the New Year, but although I tried to spend more time at his side I failed miserably. No matter what I suggested, he wriggled away somehow, his excuses feeble but, nevertheless, excuses. And, as always, that black-browed shadow on our lives was close behind him, never allowing us a moment alone.

The letter to my father was written soon after my new friend departed for Voorne, but it was some weeks before I could send it. In late December there are not many ships braving the rough waters, and it was not until one came to us, bringing me gifts for the New Year from my father himself and from my brother Edward, that I was able to dispatch it to him.

With the gifts came a long letter for me from my father, full of news, much of it news that stirred me in various ways. He was still in the north when he wrote it, having spent the months since his return to England subduing the rebellious Scots. A major victory at Falkirk had decimated and scattered Wallace's forces so thoroughly that most of ours were able to go home sometime in September, but my father had decided to remain in that part of the country till the New Year.

"You will be sorry to hear," he wrote, "that the Earl of Hereford died on the thirtieth day of November. We were good friends again, I am glad to say, for he fought gallantly and bravely all through our Scottish campaign. Young Humphrey steps into his shoes and will, I hope, fill them honorably and well."

I remember putting the letter down, after reading this, unable for some time to go any further. Humphrey, the Earl of Essex and Hereford—England's hereditary Constable and one of its most powerful and highest-ranking noblemen! My heart swelled at the thought, then turned cold, as I told myself he would undoubtedly now consider it his duty to marry. Perhaps he already had; perhaps my father would mention it on the last page—

Picking it up again, my eye suddenly caught the word "marriage." No, it was not Humphrey; it was my father himself, finally arranging, he said, his much-discussed marriage with the Lady Margaret, sister of King Philip of France.

What I felt then I find hard to describe. My dear sire had mourned our mother so deeply and for so long that the prospect of his wedding anyone, and particularly a girl my own age, disturbed and distressed me. What happiness could there be in such a union for either of them? Again, as when I first heard of Eleanora's death, I longed to be with Meg, to share with her this fresh piece of family news. Then I cheered myself by thinking that many royal marriages never came about and determining not to fret about it until it actually happened.

That, at least, was what I determined. When night fell, however, and I retired to my bed, I found it was not so easy to control my thoughts; first I pictured my father marrying his youthful French bride, then Humphrey exchanging vows with some suitable, wealthy, beautiful noblewoman, and eventually ended by crying myself to sleep.

✗

Our winter was long and very cold, with more snow than usual and so much violent wind that I was not surprised to have the weeks slip away without receiving an answer to my letter. Lord de Voorne rode into The Hague several times, I remember, seeking me out to learn whether I had heard from my father, and each time I had to say no. Then, when the weather moderated at last and I did receive a letter, there was no way to let him know.

Not that the delay made any difference! My father said nothing to ease my mind or Lord de Voorne's. There was little he could do at this particular moment, he wrote, to take from Wolphard de Borsolen the power he had placed in his hands. The cost of subduing Wallace and his followers had been enough to discourage another expedition into foreign parts, and in any case he was now deep in negotiations with France that should lead to a lasting peace. His marriage to the Lady Margaret was part of this, and so was the betrothal of my brother Edward to King Philip's daughter, the Lady Isabel.

"I find it hard to believe," he ended, "that matters are as desperate as you and Lord de Voorne seem to think. You are very young, my daughter, and you have perhaps not yet learned that people always grumble about taxes and that the man who holds the reins is often called a 'despot' and 'tyrant' by those under his rule. Be patient, Elizabeth, and we will all hope that eventually your lord nusband will grow in wisdom so that he, with you beside him, may govern his own people himself."

Just when I was finally able to show this letter to Lord de Voorne I cannot now recall, but I think it must have been in late spring. I do know it was such a warm, sunny day that after he read it we strolled together in a beautiful grove that was part of the palace parkland and, because my ladies followed very slowly behind us, we found it possible to talk freely.

"I need not tell you, my lady, how disappointed I am in King Edward's reply," he said to me immediately, his face showing his concern. "I understand, of course, why he cannot come to Holland himself, but I am extremely disturbed at the manner in which he brushes aside our difficulties."

"I'm afraid it is because I was the one who wrote him about them," I answered sadly. "Read it again and you will see that he thinks I am making too much of our people's discontent—that my youth and ignorance make me exaggerate."

Nodding, he smiled wryly down into my face. "Indeed, my lady, I do see that. I should not have asked you to do it, but I thank you for trying. It seemed to me—but never mind that now. I will write him myself and tell him that the winter months have made matters worse, not better, and I shall have some of our other nobles sign the letter with me."

We were deep in the woods by now and, as he finished speaking, we neared a small clearing. There, cropping the lush grass, stood a pretty spotted doe and her young hart, too occupied to hear our quiet footsteps. While we stood watching them a brown rabbit hopped in from the trees and, ears erect and soft nose quivering, began eating his own meal a yard or so away.

Then, behind us, one of my ladies laughed loudly enough to startle them and all three animals, after one frightened glance in our direction, turned and fled. As their bobbing white tails disappeared into a thicket, I gave a deep sigh.

"It is so peaceful, so beautiful here," I said to my companion, "that I could almost believe my father. Perhaps we *are* making too much of this problem."

"When I am home in Voorne, with the sea so close and water surrounding my holdings in every other direction, I confess I feel the same way. Voorne is really an island, you know, and it is only too easy for islanders to shut out the rest of the world and its troubles. But when I venture forth I hear from everyone I meet that this state of affairs cannot continue; as you know, my lady, my sympathy is

with them, not with my lady's father, and I'm afraid that
I must soon forget the relationship between us and join
openly in the protests against him."

This disturbing conversation remained very much on
my mind, and I decided I must somehow warn Jan and
urge him at least to try to halt Wolphard's despotism.
Surely he could do something—he was, after all, Holland's
Earl!

But the spring ended and summer was upon us and my
lord did not come to The Hague or send me any word of
any kind. Then in early August he and Lord de Vere appeared at last, riding in late one evening and, before I could
even ask for a private interview, leaving again the next
day.

By this time I was actually frightened, for I was now
hearing of the rising unrest all over Holland from a new
lady of mine—Gretchen, the Lady de Saux—a Hollander
so unlike the other members of my household that I still
wonder why Lord de Vere allowed her near me. She had
a quick mind and a warm heart and was young enough to
be a friend; and, oh, how much I needed a friend!

Once the subject had been broached between us we
talked of little else; every day brought fresh news, every
night more hours of anxiety. Embittered as I was by my
lord's neglect, I actually began to wonder if I might not be
justified in seeking shelter with Meg at Brabant or in returning to England. I was not wanted here, I told myself; I
was given no part in Holland's public affairs, I was living
in virtual retirement, and although no one could say I was
a prisoner I certainly often felt like one!

The heat, that August, was unusually oppressive, and
this, as always, made everything worse. Even with an easy

mind I would have slept little; in the circumstances, I lay awake hour after hour trying to decide what I should do.

How many restless nights I spent in this fashion I do not know, but I shall never forget how soundly I slept when I suddenly made up my mind that my duty lay here in the household set up for me by my husband. No matter what our private situation, in the eyes of the world I was the Countess of Holland, and whether my lord wanted me there or not, my place was at his side should he need me.

I awakened the next morning so refreshed and peaceful that even word of the imminent arrival of Jan and Lord de Vere did not disturb me too deeply. As usual they paid little attention to me after our formal greetings, but they did invite my ladies and me to join them at dinner the following day.

It seemed to me, when I took my seat between them, that Lord de Vere's dark countenance looked uglier and grimmer than I had ever seen it. The lines that ran from his large nose to his unsmiling lips had deepened, his scowl was more frightening, and there was such a savage gleam in his small black eyes that I feared, at first, he was angry with me.

As soon as the babble of talk around us rose, I leaned toward Jan and spoke in a voice just above a whisper.

"What is the matter with Lord de Vere? Have I annoyed him?"

"No, no," he replied hastily, keeping his own voice low. "He's disturbed because our people cannot understand why he must impose certain taxes. *I* can see why," he added, sounding pleased with himself, "but they are just too stupid!"

His words and complacent manner made my heart sink;

I could see that it would be impossible to convince him that the Hollanders were right and that we were all dangerously near disaster. How cleverly Lord de Vere handled Jan, I told myself. How could I, or anyone else, combat that cleverness?

I was quiet for a moment, watching that foolish, self-satisfied expression on my husband's young face. Then I turned back to Lord de Vere.

"Will you be remaining with us long, my lord?" I asked, for lack of anything better to say.

He shrugged. "A few days, perhaps. My plans are uncertain."

Feeling that I had done my share in beginning a conversation, I waited for him to carry it further. When he did not I mentally shrugged my own shoulders, picked up a chicken wing, and took a bite or two, determined to enjoy my dinner if nothing else.

I was about to speak to Jan again when I saw our steward hurrying down the center of the hall toward our table. He came directly to Lord de Vere and handed him a letter.

"Forgive me, my lord, for interrupting your dinner, but the courier insisted that I give this to you immediately. It comes from the Lady de Voorne."

Wolphard grunted and, while Jan and I watched him, began to read it. After the first moment or two his swarthy face darkened then paled. "The traitor!" he snarled. "The dirty, traitorous dog!"

Jan leaned over in front of me. "What is it, sir?"

Striking the letter with one hand, de Vere crushed it and threw it on the rush-covered floor.

"It's de Voorne," he replied furiously, "my daughter's

husband. She writes me that he's inciting all Holland to revolt, and she thinks he is coming here with hundreds of armed men to kill me. I must flee the country, she says!"

"Mother of God!" My lord was now paler than his guardian. "She is right! Go, dear sir, immediately! Remember how they tortured and killed my father—go now!" He rose, looking frantically around the hall as if for help. "Take some of our strongest men and go!"

While Jan was behaving like a barnyard cock in fear of its neck, Lord de Vere reached down for the letter and read it again. Then he rose, too. "Be quiet, Jan!" he said in a low voice that made the shivers run up and down my spine. "Control yourself. Do you want your people here to think you a witless coward? Come!"

And without another word he stepped from the dais and made his way through the hall with my thoroughly frightened and cowed young husband trotting at his heels like an obedient dog. Everyone at our table was watching, of course, for although Wolphard had spoken softly, Jan had not; how much the rest of the household, sitting at the other tables, had heard, I could not tell, but the usual babble died to a low murmur and their eyes followed the two men as they moved swiftly to the door.

Before they reached it I sprang to my own feet and sped after them, disregarding the curious stares that now followed *me*. I caught up with Jan in the empty antechamber and clutched his arm.

"I *must* know what is happening," I whispered urgently. "I'm your wife, Jan, and I will not be pushed aside!"

Lord de Vere glanced over his shoulder and frowned at us, but he said nothing until we entered his privy chamber.

"This does not concern you, my lady," he then announced briskly. "You will be quite safe here at The Hague. Now return to your ladies, please, and remain with them."

"No, my lord, I will not!" I replied as bravely as I could. "My lord and I are the Earl and Countess of Holland, and if our people are rebelling, as I have indeed heard they are, we should learn why and try to mend matters. Do not leave us, Lord de Vere, without telling me how I may help my lord to make his peace with our people."

"Your lord goes with me to Zealand, so you need think no more about it. Bid him farewell; we have little time to waste."

Appalled, I looked from his dark, ugly face to Jan's weak, handsome one, then back again.

"But why should Jan leave The Hague? *He* is not responsible for this trouble! No one will harm *him*." I moved closer to Jan and took his damp, trembling hand in mine. "Don't go, my lord, don't go!" I pleaded. "Stay here with me and we'll talk to the leaders of this revolt together. All will be well if we listen to their demands and behave fairly to them. Prove you are a man, Jan, and stay here!"

Gulping nervously, Jan's blue eyes met mine, then shifted to his guardian. "But I don't know—" he faltered.

"Be quiet, Jan!" Wolphard interrupted him impatiently. "You go with me! I don't want to hear another word from either of you, so go and ready yourself. Bring only what you can carry in a saddlebag and join me in the courtyard immediately. Off, now!"

With a last feeble, apologetic smile, Jan tried to free his hand from mine. But I clasped it closer. "Don't do it!" I begged him again. "If they catch you with Lord de

Vere they might well kill you both! Let him run like the rat he is and remain with me. Come, the palace is full of loyal people who will protect us and prevent him from carrying you away. All we have to do is walk out that door and shout for help."

With a smothered oath Wolphard reached my side and jerked me away from my husband, handling me with a roughness that was truly frightening. "I've had more than enough of your interference," he told me grimly and, before I could protest, marched me swiftly into his bed-chamber and threw me on the bed.

"These walls are thick," he said "Scream until you are hoarse and no one will hear you!"

A moment later the door slammed behind him, and, in the sudden silence, I heard a key turn in the lock.

Eighteen

I was on my feet and banging my fists on the door a moment later, calling for help as loudly as I could. Nothing happened, however, and after my voice grew hoarse and my hands wearied and bruised, I knelt down and tried to peer through the keyhole. But the key must have been left in it, and, realizing that Lord de Vere's apartments were always kept for his use and that if he had, indeed, left the palace, the servants might not enter them for days, I sat down on a chest and struggled to regain my composure.

As the feeling of panic subsided, I glanced around the small chamber. It was a windowless closet, holding a bed and the chest on which I was perched, and that was all. For some time I just sat there, my only concern how to escape from my prison; then I began to think of Wolphard's treatment of me and to hope that he would soon be caught.

But Jan—what of Jan? Were the Hollanders angry enough to kill their own young Earl, or were they aware that he was only de Vere's tool and should not be held responsible for his despotic rule? Foolish as he was, weak as he was, despite his neglect of me, I found I could not bear the thought of poor Jan being maimed, mutilated, slain, as his father was before him. I had once seen a soft rabbit caught in a trap, its pink eyes wild, its hind feet pounding madly, and I had heard strange, unearthly screams coming from its throbbing throat. Just so, I was sure, would my young husband behave. . . .

Again my heart jumped into my throat and a fresh feeling of panic surged over me. I *must* get out, I told myself, I *must* get out and save Jan somehow! But how? How? As I rose, determined to bang and scream even louder than before, my robe brushed against a silver ewer and basin on the chest beside me.

There was water in the ewer. Without wasting a moment, I poured it on the stone floor, snatched up the basin, ran back to the door, and beat the basin with ewer, making wonderful, bell-like sounds that all but deafened me.

How long I kept up my mad clamor I do not know. To make so much noise, both basin and ewer were, of course, of very heavy silver and my hands and arms were already sore and tired. Just as I thought I could not knock them together one more time, the door suddenly opened and there stood Lady Gretchen de Saux, her arms outstretched.

"Oh, my lady, my lady!" was all she could say, over and

over, while I threw those two utensils down and fell on her neck.

"Thank God, thank God, thank God!" was all I could reply.

"We've been searching the whole palace," she said at last. "Then the stupid guard in this corridor remembered seeing you enter these apartments with the lord Earl and Lord de Vere, and when I ran in I heard something and saw the key in the door—"

"Lord de Vere locked me in," I explained. "I tried to detain my lord—oh, Gretchen, he should not have gone! He should not have gone! They may kill him! Come, we must send after them—"

Without thinking what I was doing, I rushed out through the antechamber, past the open-mouthed, staring guard, never pausing until I reached the Great Hall. Once inside I halted, breathless. Surely here I would find someone to help; it was always a busy place, with our people and friends coming and going.

Today, except for a servant or two lurking in the corners and a dog rooting through the rushes, it was empty.

I turned, desperate, and all but stepped on Gretchen, who was right behind me. "Where is everyone?" I wailed. "I need help! My lord must be rescued! Oh, God, *where is everyone?*"

Back down the corridor I ran, with Gretchen pounding after me; it was even emptier than the Great Hall and, as I ran, the terrors of the last hour or so overwhelmed me. I lost the last of my composure and, I am ashamed to confess, I began to weep. Loud sobs choked me; then I heard myself screaming, calling Wolphard names.

"He's a beast, a coward, a traitor! And they'll blame Jan—poor Jan—"

Lady de Saux caught hold of me and tried to pull me to one side, but I paid no attention to her. Finally something she was repeating broke through my mad panic.

"Look down into the courtyard, my lady, look! It is crowded with people! Look down into the courtyard!"

Listening, at last, I followed her to the window. As she had said, the cobbled enclosure below us was alive with men and women all gathered around a band of horsemen, still on their mounts. Everyone seemed to be waving their hands and shouting to each other, but I could not hear what they were saying.

For a minute or two we stood and stared at them. "Should you hide, my lady?" asked Gretchen, sounding frightened.

"Why? I've done nothing."

She was still regarding me with anxious eyes when the sound of loud footsteps on the stairs reached our ears. I remained where I was as they approached, determined to show no fear no matter what happened. Drawing myself up to my fullest height, I smiled encouragingly at Gretchen and waited.

A moment later two men appeared, striding swiftly toward me. I gave a great sigh of relief, for although one was a stranger the other—and oh, how grateful I was!—was Lord de Voorne.

"Thank God you are here, my lady!" he exclaimed fervently, dropping on one knee before me. "Your people told me you had disappeared."

"Lord de Vere locked me in his apartments before he

fled from the palace," I explained. "And Lady de Saux here only now discovered where I was and released me." Putting out my hands, I clasped his warmly. "Oh, dear Lord de Voorne, we must try to rescue my poor husband! That vile man would not let him remain here with me. I tried, believe me, I tried!"

"We must indeed. In fact, we came to you because we want your help in doing so, for if de Vere takes your lord out of Holland, my lady, he may never be allowed to return. I have a band of armed men with me, but we must rouse the townspeople, too, so come to the market place, if you will, and appeal to them. They will listen to *you*, my lady! Come, before it is too late!"

I needed no urging; I was running toward the stairs while he was still speaking, leaving them to hurry after me. Except for a guard or two I saw no one until I stepped out into the courtyard. Pausing there, just outside the huge doorway, I called to the crowd gathered on the cobbles, clapping my hands for silence.

"We go to rescue my lord husband," I shouted as loudly as I could. "The Lord de Vere has taken him prisoner! For my sake, good people, for your young Earl, for Holland, find weapons and follow us!"

They cheered and made way for me. Still running, I sped across the courtyard, over the drawbridge, past the peaceful lake, and through the quiet streets to The Hague's center. Faces appeared at windows, doors opened, and, as I continued to call out my plea for help, many of the inhabitants of the houses I was passing rushed out and joined the growing mass following me.

By the time I reached the market place I had almost lost what was left of my voice, and the tears were again streaming down my cheeks. I cannot remember what I said to the people who streamed in from all four sides, shoving each other aside to listen. I just know that I begged them to save Jan from the man they now hated and that wild cheers went up as I did so.

All was confusion. Before I knew what was happening someone tossed me up on a horse, Gretchen on another. More horses appeared like magic; men by the dozens climbed into their saddles, women ran back and forth carrying weapons to them, children shouted excitedly, dogs barked.

Suddenly a trumpet blared, and in the silence that fell Lord de Voorne's voice rang out. "Follow me, my friends! They left by the west gate and have been seen on the coast road!"

As we pounded out of the square and through the narrow streets I found myself riding beside Lord de Voorne, the two of us leading the small army behind us. It never occurred to me not to go with them, and it was not until we came to the first bridge along the way that anyone suggested I should return to the palace.

They had good reason, for Wolphard had torn down the bridge facing us. While I sat in my saddle staring at his wanton destruction, Lord de Voorne spoke briefly to some of the other men, then to me.

"They have at least an hour's start, my lady, and now this—" He waved at the depressing sight in front of us. "We will press on, but we may never overtake them now! Go home—two of our party will escort you and Lady de Saux—and I will send you word at the first possible moment."

I shook my head. "Please let me ride on a little farther,"

I said. "It must have taken them some time to tear down the bridge. They may not be too far ahead."

After a slight argument he agreed and we galloped on. But when we came to the next bridge and found Wolphard had destroyed that one as well, I had to turn very stubborn and refuse flatly to go home.

I will not describe in detail the delays and horrors of that wild ride. It would have been frightening enough to think of poor Jan in that man's hands without these indisputable signs of his ruthless determination to foil any attempt at a rescue; as it was, each ruined bridge, and there were several, made me feel more strongly that we must somehow save Jan.

I have since wondered why I cared. I still do not know. Perhaps because we had been children together there was some affection for him deep in a corner of my heart. Who knows? In the circumstances I might well have been relieved to have Jan removed forcibly from my life; whatever the reason, I was not.

The fact that we were never in any doubt as to which way Wolphard's party was fleeing helped us very much. Fortunately it was the kind of hot summer day that took people out into the fields, and there was always someone who had seen them. The ruined bridges, of course, were visible proof that we were on his trail.

There was little doubt, too, but that Wolphard was heading for a spot where he could find a ship to take them from Holland, and before long we realized that it must be Maassluis, a fishing village and river port near the sea.

But by the time we rode down to the small harbor I knew we were too late. There was no one there except a few fishermen, mending their nets, and some boys splashing around in the shallow waves creaming up on the sand.

Then Lord de Voorne, who had pulled up his mount beside mine, pointed out to sea. "Look!" he said. "That ship—it's becalmed! I wonder—" He swung himself out of the saddle, threw his reins to me, and strode over to the nearest fisherman.

He was back a moment later, his face glowing with excitement. "They are on that ship!" he shouted to the rest of our band, now gathered around me and Gretchen. "Sailing for Sweden! Come, we'll take these boats and row out. Unless a wind comes up, we have them!"

Cheering and shouting the men obeyed him, leaving only two grooms to take care of the horses. They ran to the beached boats and, in less time than it takes to tell it, were moving swiftly over the quiet water.

I sat and watched, my heart pounding. The ship was well out into the harbor, but I could see its sails flapping idly in the dead calm and, on the deck, a group of men. If Wolphard and Jan were among them, and I was sure they were, I could imagine the agony they must be undergoing as they saw the fleet of boats skimming over the glassy surface toward them.

Even a whisper of breeze would save them, for the fishing boats were small and many of the men at their oars were unskilled. It was obvious, even to me, that we could not catch the ship once it got under way.

As our brave Hollanders neared the rolling, helpless vessel, I heard myself praying out loud. "No wind, dear God, no wind! Please, dear God, please—"

I suppose that Jan must be praying, too, but how different *his* prayers would be!

I stopped praying to give a cry of joy. They were there! They were surrounding the ship! I could actually see our men waving their weapons and hear them shouting something to the men gathered on the deck. While I sat clutching the pommel of my saddle, my legs trembling, I heard more shouting back and forth out there on the water. Then, finally, a dark-haired figure climbed slowly down the side of the larger vessel and dropped into one of the waiting boats close at its side.

With flashing oars it moved away and another took its place. A second figure, tall, slender, with fair hair that gleamed in the sunlight, appeared at the rail. Instead of descending, he remained there and the shouting started again.

It had to be Jan, I told myself. Why was he delaying; what would keep him on the ship now? At last, however, he moved to the rope ladder, and as he, in his turn, dropped into the bobbing boat under it, the greatest cheer of all went up from the waiting rescuers.

It was echoed by the two grooms beside me on the strand; I tried to shout with them, but a great sob rose in my throat, and to my astonishment I found I was weeping.

Nineteen

I stood beside my lord on the dais while his uncle, John d'Avennes, the Earl of Hainault, was being invested as his new Regent, and for the first time I felt I was truly what my recently made seal called me: "Elizabeth, Countess of Holland and Zealand, and Lady of Friesland."

We had come to Dort to welcome Earl John; to my great relief, there was no suggestion by anyone that I should remain in seclusion at The Hague. Indeed, from the day of Jan's rescue I had been included in every meeting of his council, and my name was signed after my husband's on any document of importance.

And, although Jan was most reluctant at first to return to The Hague with me after leaving that ship, we had since become better friends. Perhaps because he was told of the part I played in saving him from exile with Wolphard de Borsolen; perhaps because he thought that, were he not wed to a daughter of England, he might have been put to death, too, when Lord de Vere was, later that day, by our angry people.

Or it may have been just Jan's way of falling in with whatever was easiest for him. When the Earl of Hainault was chosen for his guardian in de Vere's place, he agreed warmly; he seemed to welcome my presence at his side, and he not only approved of my having a seal of my own, he actually came to my privy chamber to watch the artist making the sketch for it, first complimenting me on the tight-sleeved tunic and miniver-lined mantle I had chosen to wear and then, with gentle fingers, coaxing my little falcon to perch quietly on my wrist.

I thought of that moment as we took our part in the regency ceremony, and it gave me fresh hope for our future life together. I was, in fact, thinking just that when I looked over at Earl John and saw him smiling at me.

No one, certainly, could have been more unlike dark, ugly Wolphard than this short, stout uncle of Jan's. He had a most benign countenance with twinkling blue eyes, a button nose, and a trim little silver beard: a man to be loved but, as I had already discovered, a man to be respected, for behind the merry eyes was a mind that was wise and a will that was firm.

With him to guide us for the next four years we might well, at the end of that time, be ready and able to assume our real duties as Earl and Countess of Holland.

Cheered by this prospect, I watched Jan sign the regency contract. It being my turn next, I took his place at the table and reached for the pen.

"Read it first, my lady," said the Earl of Hainault, before I dipped the pen in the ink. "Never write your name on anything you have not read."

As I bent my head to obey, I saw Jan looking very surprised. I knew why: in the long months of Lord de Vere's rule he had never allowed Jan to read the many documents issued in his name and had kept Jan's seal in his own hands to use whenever he wished.

This particular deed was long, but I skimmed through it all, from its beginning—"We, John, Earl of Holland and Zealand, and Lord of Friesland, and we, Elizabeth, Countess and Lady of the same places—" to the closing phrase that read, "These letters are made at the petition of my dear lords and my beloved wife, on this day, the vigils of St. Jude, October 27, 1299."

Then, happier than I had ever been since my arrival in Holland, I signed my name with a flourish, affixed my seal, and handed it to our new Regent.

A minute or two later, my lord and I were standing side by side again while our uncle stepped forward to receive the homage of our nobles. It was apparent that they were more than content with Wolphard's successor, and, when the last of them bent his knee and promised his fealty, a great cheer rang through the hall. It was a heart-warming moment, and one I will never forget; nor, indeed, will I ever forget what Earl John said to all of us as soon as the huge chamber became silent enough for his voice to be heard.

"The task that I take upon myself today, my lords, is, as you know, not an easy one. The people of Holland are unhappy—and rightly so, for they have been very badly treated. Therefore, we must waste not an hour in both allaying their fears for the future and righting the wrongs of the past. With the understanding and agreement of my dearest nephew, I shall take the first steps to do this immediately."

He paused, cleared his throat, then continued. "Your young Earl has had a sad and frightening experience. He has been deceived by a man he was told to trust and obey, a man who won his heart and then took every possible advantage of his youth and affection. That man is dead. We, the living, must prove to our people that his wicked deeds died with him."

Turning back to us, he took Jan by the hand and led him to the front of the dais. "Tell our friends, my lord, what you and I have agreed on this day."

Jan, his face flushed, replied in his usual hesitant manner. "In fairness to our people, we shall deprive Lord de Vere's heirs of his ill-gotten gains, and we hereby also revoke every state deed passed since the death of my beloved father."

While another great cheer rose from the crowd, Earl John gave Jan an encouraging smile and the two of them moved to the table where we had signed the contract of regency. When they reached it, our uncle picked up two or three seals that were on it.

"Here," he announced, waving one of them in his right hand, "is your Earl's new seal, which you saw him use today for the first time." He handed it to Jan and held out the other one so we could all see it. "And this is the seal that Lord de Vere took from him to authenticate those evil state deeds just now revoked. It is my nephew's wish, and mine, that it be broken in your presence, never to be used again."

A servant appeared on the dais with a hammer; a sharp blow shattered the seal into little pieces.

"From this moment on," said Earl John, speaking over the sounds of approval from the onlookers, "your lord Earl and I, as his Regent, will sign both our names to every document and affix both our seals. The days of tyranny and despotism here in Holland are, I promise you, forever over!"

✶

After this stirring scene ended, Jan's uncle went quietly to work with our nobles, making fair laws, reducing taxes, doing as speedily as possible what was needed to restore Holland to its peaceful state.

Jan and I were often present, I am delighted to say, and nothing could have been more harmonious than the way every problem was soon solved. My one regret was that Lord de Voorne, who was really more responsible than anyone else for this happy entente, could not be a member of our council. But because of the execution of his wife's father and because she and his own child had had to be disinherited, this obviously could not be arranged.

He pointed this out himself, saying that he would, for a while anyway, remain in Voorne, leaving the reforms in Earl John's hands.

So much was accomplished so quickly that when Jan grew restless and asked, a little timidly, if he might ride up to Haarlem for some hunting, his uncle encouraged him to do so. Then, to my surprise, he turned to me.

"Go with the lad, my lady," he suggested. "You have both suffered much in recent weeks, and I see no reason why you should not now enjoy a change of air and occupation. Go, and be sure that I will take care of Holland's affairs in your absence."

Whether Jan wanted me with him I do not know; he was all that was friendly and courteous, but after we arrived at his hunting lodge I saw him only at meals. The long days in the saddle made him sleepy, and there was no entertainment in the evenings; life here was simple, and my ladies and I were left to amuse ourselves as best we could.

In any case it was an interval in which I recovered fully from the horrors of Jan's abduction and rescue, and one night, when heavy rains had put an end to his sport, I found myself quite willing to play merels with him after supper, a game we had sometimes enjoyed together during our childhood.

Unfortunately I won too often that first evening, so, instead of continuing our contest the following night, he lingered at the table, drinking more and more wine until he was drunk and quarrelsome. I suppose I should have retired and left him to it, but thinking I might help matters, I remained. At first he was merely surly and difficult to talk to; then, to my great distress, he began to mutter to himself, abusing his uncle, Earl John.

"I will *not* be treated like a child again!" I heard him say, his voice thick and an ugly scowl on his face. "I am Earl here. I won't have him signing things!"

"But, my lord," I broke in, "you were quite content with the way everything was arranged when we left home. You know that our Regent is ruling Holland *with* you; you both sign your names to every state paper. Lord de Vere never let you read them when you signed them! And have you forgotten that he affixed your seal with his own hand?"

Jan turned on me furiously. "And why was that, my lady? Because I was fool enough to obey *your father!* Someone is always telling me what to do, and I'm tired of it! I'm tired of it, do you hear? I am the Earl, and it is time everyone knew it!"

With a sweeping gesture he knocked over his wine, rose unsteadily, and pushed back his chair, overturning it in the process. Then, while I sat and watched him, he stalked out of the hall, still muttering to himself.

I thought all this would be forgotten after a night's sleep, but much the same scene was repeated the next evening, with Jan sounding even angrier and more resentful. When I tried to reason with him again he told me, in front of the whole table, to mind my own affairs and allow him to settle his.

"I don't want any help from you *or* your royal father! Or from my high and mighty uncle, either. And if you think I'm just talking, my lady, you wait and see! I wrote Earl John this morning, telling him that I would rule Holland from now on and that he could pack up his belongings and go home to Hainault."

I said nothing. What was there to say? What could I do? And what, I asked myself, could I *ever* do with this stupid, willful, weak, childish husband of mine? Here he was, only a week after agreeing happily and enthusiastically to Earl John's regency, wanting to overturn everything—and for no reason that I could think of except his silly vacillation and pride.

Later I wondered if I should not have written Earl John, too, and urged him to come to us immediately. But I was so sure that that was what he would do the moment he received Jan's letter that I did nothing. Instead, he summoned Jan to Dort.

"We will discuss the regency again, my dear nephew," he wrote. "If you and our nobles feel you are ready to take the reins in your own hands, I will be happy to relinquish them to you."

Jan showed this to me and, smiling triumphantly, his reply. "He hopes to lure me there and kill me," he told me. "I am not that much of a fool, I promise you. Read this."

His was, needless to say, a badly written, misspelled document, the work of a suspicious boy living in a confused world. The gist of it was this: "I will certainly not come to Dort. Meet me at Rotterdam under the safeguard of a truce. I will be attended by not more than one hundred men-at-arms, and I want your assurance that your entourage will not outnumber mine."

Earl John's response to it was brief. "Where there is no enmity, my lord, there is no need of a truce."

Later I heard that our nobles, exasperated by Jan's change of face, offered to accompany Earl John to Rotterdam with every knight and man-at-arms they could raise, but Earl John refused. "No, no," he said to them, "we must not allow my nephew to draw us into any real conflict. I will wait until he comes to me. If I am patient he will change his mind again."

✳

While our Regent was doing his best to prevent Jan from making a public fool of himself, Jan's imagined grievances, fed by wine, grew nightly. "He is afraid of me," was one of his favorite remarks, made much too often and much too loudly at the high table. "He knows my people want *me*, not him! If he refuses once more to meet me at Rotterdam, I shall march down to Dort and tear up that regency contract in the market square."

What I was feeling at this time can be imagined. I tried whenever possible to calm him down, but my attempts to do so were met with such hostility that I finally decided I was merely making matters worse. And when we heard that Earl John was called to Hainault on urgent family business, I think I was actually relieved, hoping that by the time he returned Jan might well be busying himself over something else.

This, I recollect, was about the seventh or eighth day of November. The weather cleared; Jan spent a long day in the saddle again and, after a most successful hunting expedition, joined us at supper in a sunny humor, talking only of the great sport he had just enjoyed. He drank little although he ate voraciously. I commented on it when he called for a fresh platter of eels and heaped a huge serving—his third—in front of him.

He grimaced. "I'm still hungry," he said, "and that last serving tasted a bit tainted." A large mouthful brought back the smile to his face. "Good," he remarked contentedly. "Do have some. You won't get eels like these any place but Holland!"

✳

I wakened the next morning to see patches of sunshine on the stone floor. "My lord will hunt today," I told Gretchen as we broke our fast. "Thank the good God for that—another peaceful supper for us all."

But she shook her head. "I'm afraid not, my lady. They tell me he is unwell—his bowels, I believe."

"Oh?" I was surprised. Jan was rarely ill. "I'll send a

woman to him with a mixture I brought from England. It will put him right in no time."

I was, in fact, so sure it would that I was astonished to find his chair empty at dinner and supper, and then again at dinner the following day. Our chamberlain informed me in a very grave tone that the ailment had worsened. "My lord would not bring his physician with him, my lady," he said, "so we are searching Haarlem for anyone with some knowledge of medicine."

Later that afternoon I went to Jan's bedchamber to see for myself how he was faring. The room seemed, at first glance, to be filled with people: a stranger was bending over my lord, servants were scurrying around with utensils of various kinds, two of his gentlemen were whispering in a corner.

Approaching the bed a little timidly, for I had not had much experience with illness, I was suddenly frightened by the gauntness of his face. How could anyone change so greatly in such a short time? The bones in his cheeks, the hollows under his eyes, the pinched nostrils seemed to give him the look of an old man.

"I'm sorry to find you so miserable, my lord," I said. "Is there anything I can do for you?"

He shook his head impatiently. "Unless you know how to stop the vomiting and the flux, no."

As I stood there, trying to think of something comforting to say, the stranger—an apothecary, I learned later—came around the bed to me.

"Perhaps you can tell me, my lady. Has my lord Earl eaten anything that might cause this violent attack?"

"It's nothing I ate," interrupted Jan before I could reply.

"Why won't you believe me? I've been poisoned, I tell you—poisoned!"

"Nonsense, Jan! Who would poison you? And why?" I'm sure I sounded impatient.

"That traitor uncle of mine, of course. He wants Holland, and I'm in his way." My lord's voice grew shriller with each word, his eyes wilder, and his hands, which he waved as he talked, began to tremble. Beads of sweat formed on his brow, and he vomited suddenly into a basin that lay on the covers beside him.

The apothecary held his head until the paroxysm ended, wiped his face with a damp towel, and handed the basin to a servant.

"Think, my lady," he said to me again. "What has your lord eaten in the last few days?"

The picture of Jan heaping his plate with eels flashed into my mind. "Eels," I said. "Remember, my lord? You said they tasted tainted and sent for a fresh platter."

He glared at me. "It was not the eels, I tell you. I have been poisoned. Now leave me alone and let me rest."

I saw him turn his head away and close his eyes, so I obeyed without another word. When I reached the door I found the apothecary beside me.

"He is not himself or he would not make such a wild accusation," I whispered. "My lord of Hainault is the most honorable of men and has been exceedingly kind to us."

"Of course, my lady, of course! These are the fancies of a very ill young man—and he is, I am afraid, very ill indeed. Tainted eels could certainly be the cause of it, but how to halt this continuing vomit and flux I do not know.

It has gone on so long now that your lord is sadly weakened; the potions we always use seem ineffective; but at his age, his strength will surely return."

There was something in his tone and in his face, however, that belied his final words, and I returned to my apartments with such a sense of foreboding that I summoned our chamberlain.

"I am not happy about my lord Earl's condition," I told him. "Nor is the apothecary. Should we not try to find a physician as well to help him?"

"I have already sent a squire to The Hague for our own man of medicine, my lady, with orders to ride day and night," he replied.

When I was told that the physician had come and was with Jan, my anxiety lessened, and as the hour was late I went to bed, hoping for better news in the morning. How long I slept I am not sure, but I remember a voice calling me and someone shaking me. Through the mists of slumber came the words, "Wake up, my lady, wake up! Your lord wants you! Your lord wants you!"

I sat bolt upright and saw Gretchen de Saux hovering over me with my chamber robe.

"Here," she said urgently, "wrap this around you and come with me."

A moment later we were hurrying through the dark corridors to Jan's apartments, led by one of his gentlemen carrying a flare.

Gretchen shook her head when I asked her what was happening. "All I know is that the Earl wants you."

This time Jan's bedchamber was quite orderly; the confusion and bustle had passed and the only thing that broke the night quiet was the terrifying sound of his labored breathing. A dim figure or two stood near the bed, and as I approached one of them moved forward to meet me.

"What is it?" I whispered. "Is he worse?"

"He is sinking fast," was the hushed reply. "He asked for you a short time ago, but whether he will rouse now I do not know. Go to him, my lady, and hold his hand in yours. The warmth may reach him."

Choking back a sob, I hastened over and knelt on the floor, leaning on the side of the high bed. Jan's hand lay on the coverlet, and I took it in mine, clasping it closely.

"Jan," I said softly. "Jan—Jan—"

His fingers stirred; then, after a minute, I saw his eyelids quiver, open, then close again.

"Bette?" It was a long time since he had called me that, and the sound of it, in a thread of a voice, almost his old, little-boy voice, brought the tears to my eyes in a sudden rush. "Bette?"

"Yes, Jan. I'm here."

"I feel strange—strange, Bette. And there's no one—I thought perhaps you would come—"

"I wanted to, Jan. Don't talk now; just rest. I'll hold your hand and we'll remember the happy days in England when we played together."

"I'd—like that. The happy days—"

As he fell silent, I began to murmur about the sunny gardens at Langley, the meadows where we hawked, the firelit hall where we learned to dance in the long winter evenings. He sighed, once or twice, but it seemed to me that his breathing eased and I had a flash of hope. The physician *must* be wrong. Jan could not be dying. Jan was too young to die! I would lull him to sleep by talking very, very softly, and he would awaken refreshed and stronger.

I whispered on and on: Windsor, the tiltyard, Edward, the dogs. . . .

The fingers in mine grew cooler, so I held them even more closely. That, I told myself, would warm them again. They *were* warmer, they were! They had to be, they—

A gentle hand touched my shoulder. "Come, my lady," said someone. "Come with me."

Twenty

$\mathcal{I}$ signed the last document, shook sand over the wet ink, affixed my seal, and handed it to Earl John—now, of course, the Earl of Holland as well as the Earl of Hainault. He placed it with the others and gave me a warm smile.

"So, my dear child. Our work is done at last. Now, before I set out for Hainault again, tell me what I may do for you?"

"There is only one thing in this world that I want, my lord," was my prompt reply, "and that is to go home. Make the necessary arrangements to release my dower and let me go home!"

This particular day was, I think, in late February; and it was true that my one wish and thought during the months that had elapsed since Jan's death was to return to England. We had laid him to rest in Dort beside Earl Florence, the father he had loved so well; but although I knelt at the bier as his young widow, clad in a wife's mourning robes, the tears I shed then were not for my husband. *That* poor Jan had never been. Instead I wept for a playmate of my childhood, the small boy whose hand I held while he breathed his last.

With those tears were washed away all the unhappy memories of the difficult years in between, leaving me free to go where I wanted, do what I wanted; to begin, in fact, a new life. I even felt free to think of Humphrey in a way that had never before been possible. For the first time I allowed myself to hope that he and I might become man and wife. Why not? I had done my duty by wedding Jan; surely now I could follow my heart.

I soon learned, however, that although I was free to think as I wished, I was not yet free to go or do what I wanted. I must not leave Holland, my father wrote me, until I had secured all my rights as Countess dowager, rights that were mine for the rest of my life. At first I assumed this would be a simple matter, but I was very wrong indeed: all during December, January, and February our messengers crossed the rough winter seas, carrying my letters asking for assistance to my father and his to me, giving advice and counseling patience.

With one of his early missives came two ladies, my dear Lady Isabella de Vescy and Lady Jane Dacre, another old friend. They were sent, according to the King, "to companionate and comfort you"—which they certainly did, for they were proof to me that one of these days I would set out for home in their company, a daughter of England's King with her English ladies.

But the weeks rolled on without anything being settled; and on this late February day, when I signed my last document that concerned Holland's affairs, my own were not yet concluded. When I asked Earl John to release my dowry and let me go home, he sighed and avoided my eyes.

"I wish you were not so eager to leave us, my child," he said. "You have won Holland's heart with your courage and your beauty. Why not continue to make it your home?"

"It never *has* been my home, my lord. There has not been a day when I felt truly happy here, as I think you must know, and now my one desire is to return to England and my lord father."

"Then you shall, my lady. Money matters take time, but I will do what I can to speed you on your way."

I thanked him and took my leave, telling myself that perhaps he would. But, having learned how even the kindest and most honorable of men hate to part with money, I was not surprised as more time slipped by without anything happening. Another letter from me to my father brought two of his ablest men of business to The Hague with his reply, dated the seventeenth of March; they would help me in wresting my fortune from Earl John's reluctant hands, he wrote me, and I was to assist them in every way I could.

Needless to say I welcomed them warmly, and right there and then I placed all my documents in their hands and answered every question they could think of to ask me. Only after that did I open two other letters they brought me from England—one from my brother Edward, the second from Joanna.

Edward's said little: he looked forward to my return and gave me news of the horses and dogs I had left at Langley. Joanna's told me much more.

"Rafe is in Ireland," she said, "looking after our estates there; and I am here at Windsor during his absence, visiting our father and the Lady Margaret. You will be glad to know, Bette, that their marriage seems to be a happy one —what a fortunate man our father is!—and that they will have a child in early June. Something you may *not* be glad to hear is that he is already receiving offers for your hand. I asked him about it, after rumors reached my ears, but all he would say was that his experience with me had taught him not to let his daughters remain unmarried very long."

I remember sitting in stunned silence for some minutes, then walking frantically around the room, actually wringing my hands. What should I do? Who could I turn to for help and advice? How could I stop my father from arranging another wretched marriage for me? Perhaps it was too late; Joanna's letter had been written some weeks ago!

I was still pacing up and down when Lady Isabella de Vescy entered. One glance at me was enough to tell her that something was very wrong, and in reply to her anxious questions I handed her Joanna's letter. After she had read it I told her how unhappy I had been with Jan and that I could not bear the prospect of another such match. Of my love for Humphrey I said nothing; I had never discussed him with anyone, not even my sisters, and the fear that he was wed to someone else, perhaps, or had long forgotten me, made me continue to hold my tongue.

"Write the King," Lady Isabella suggested. "Tell him what Joanna has written you and ask him to do nothing until after you return to England. He knows how eager you are to go home; he will surely agree."

There being nothing better to do, I followed her advice and dispatched my letter at the first possible moment.

Now I watched the hours, days, and weeks pass carrying a double burden. When would I hear from my father, and when would Earl John release my dower rights?

It was the end of April, finally, and I still waited. May came and went. June—

Lady Isabella hurried in to me with a smile on her face and a letter in her hand. "At last, my child. Read it and tell me what your lord father says."

With trembling fingers I broke the seal:

My dearest daughter Elizabeth, Countess of Holland and Zealand, Lady of Friesland.

The Lady Margaret was safely delivered of a son on the first day of June. We have named him Thomas and he seems a fine, healthy boy: a fine, healthy *English* boy, for he refused the milk of a French wetnurse and screamed lustily until we found an English woman for him.

I write this from Carlisle, where our army is gathered again to quiet the Scots. Will these uprisings never end?

And now, my daughter, I send you the assurance you wish to hear. Although I have indeed given some thought to your future, I will not make any fresh arrangements for it until after your year of mourning has come to an end. By then I trust you will be home with me. In the meantime, I send you my wishes for your good health and a father's blessing.

I gave a great sigh of relief and read it aloud to Lady Isabella. For me, it was as if the sun had broken through a clouded sky, and for the next few days I felt almost care-free. Jan died on the tenth of November—and it was now only June. I had, I told myself, five months still before I need worry again.

Then, at the end of the month, my short interval of comparative tranquility ended. My father's two men of business came to me one morning looking so gloomy that my heart sank.

"Yes, gentlemen?" I said, after I had greeted them. "You need my help today?"

'I'm afraid not, my lady," was the reply. "The truth of the matter is that we have failed in our mission. We cannot force Earl John to give you your rights, and we have done all we can to urge him. It will not be easy to confess to the King that we have spent so many months here without accomplishing what we came for, but we have no hope that remaining longer would improve matters. With your permission, my lady, we will set out for home immediately."

I stared at them, aghast. I had been distressed at the passing of the weeks, but I had not thought they could fail! What was I to do now? There was no reason to think that Earl John would change his mind after their departure, and I *must* be in England before my father began arranging another marriage for me. The months that had seemed blessedly long now suddenly shrank, and I felt actual panic.

"I cannot keep you here, of course," I told them. "Give me time to write my lord father, however, and once my letter is in your hands we will say farewell. I know how difficult your task has been, and I am, believe me, exceedingly grateful for all you have tried to do for me."

With that I dismissed them. The moment they were gone I burst into tears. I had not once wept over this increasingly disturbing delay, but now, faced with the need to remain in Holland indefinitely, and realizing that if my father pledged my hand to some other foreign noble I might never reach England at all, I lost control over my emotions and gave way completely.

I was alone, for my interview with my father's men had been a private one, or I might not have done so. As it was, I sobbed wildly for a few minutes; then, after the worst of the storm had passed, I dried my eyes and forced myself to consider the problems more calmly.

Another plea to my father for help might simply result in another reply telling me to be patient. Well, I had had too many of those letters already. I had been patient, I had obeyed him in every way, and I was still trapped here in Holland. It was true that I wanted my dower rights—I needed them, in fact, for I had no other money with which to pay my household expenses if I left Earl John's protection.

I had my jewels, of course, and all my gold and silver plate. How long they would keep me, I did not know, but I doubted that my father would want me to sell them or that he would refuse to pay my people once I reached his side. Did I have enough money for the journey? Did I dare disregard his orders and set out for home without his permission? Would my ladies accompany me, knowing that they might incur his anger?

All these questions raced around in my mind; then, as I began to think a bit more sensibly, some of the answers came to me. The thing to do, I decided, was to write my father telling him that because his men had failed to help me I was returning home immediately—but not with them. My preparations would take too long for that, and I would want to break my journey in Brabant to see Meg again, if only briefly.

By the time my letter reached him, however, I would be well on my way, making it, I hoped, impossible for him to prevent my return.

Having determined to carry out this plan, I conferred with my ladies and found that not only were my English attendants perfectly agreeable but Gretchen de Saux, without a moment's hesitation, announced that she, too, would come with me.

Cheered and encouraged by this, I wrote the necessary letter, gave it to the waiting men of business, and watched them ride away. I then wrote another saying more or less the same thing and despatched it to Earl John, who had just left Holland for Hainault. That being done, we all threw ourselves into the task of deciding what possessions would go with us, what should follow later, what must be discarded.

It seemed an insurmountable chore at first, but before long the worst was over and we were bidding our friends and servants farewell. The day of our departure was, I remember, exceedingly hot; it was now July, and Holland in July can be very hot indeed. But my heart was so light, as we rode through the city gates and down the road that led to Brussels, that I welcomed it, telling myself that the warm weather would ensure us a calm voyage without the delays that would be inevitable later in the year.

We reached Brabant without incident, where we were welcomed by both Meg and Jean. For the whole of our sojourn with them they presented, even to me, the picture of a reasonably contented married couple; that this was not true I knew, of course, but I must confess that it made our visit easier and much more pleasant than I had expected when I found Jean there. He also surprised me by taking upon himself the whole problem and expense of our voyage, providing us with ships for my party and my possessions and, for the first time, behaving like an affectionate brother.

Meg, when I commented on this, gave a hard, bitter little laugh. "He hopes you will carry the s-story of his devotion to me back to our father," she said, stammering only slightly. "The truth is that he has just discarded his p-present mistress and has not yet found a new one. But do not fret over me, Bette. I grow accustomed, t-truly I do. Go home and be happy!"

Whatever his reason, Jean was unflagging in his courteous treatment of me and my ladies and gentlemen and, with Meg at his side, accompanied us to Antwerp, where we finally set sail. To my joy, we had two nights together at the Steen, the old castle on the harbor where my father and I had sought shelter back in 1298. Then, alas, my joy faded, for each time I parted with my dear sister I had that terrible fear that it might be years before we again met—if ever. And now, with the dread possibility that my father might force me into a marriage that would take me to some distant country, I had, certainly, sufficient reason to feel that fear.

Meg, I'm sure, was thinking the same thought. We kissed each other repeatedly, fighting back the tears; but as the small boat rowed me away from the shore on which she was still standing, I finally let them slip down my cheeks.

✶

Our voyage was slow and uneventful. The seas were calm—too calm, often—and the winds light. Now that I was actually on my way home, however, I was in no particular hurry to reach there. These golden days under the deep blue skies were utterly peaceful, providing me with the perfect interval in which to put behind me the lonely, miserably unhappy years of my marriage and the frustrating months of my widowhood. With each hour in the beneficent sun, watching the green water foam into white lace as our ship cut through it, I grew younger and younger, my cares and responsibilities a thing of the past, my future for now, at least, in abeyance.

Occasionally I allowed myself to dream of Humphrey, recalling in detail every moment we had spent together, every word, every kiss. But most of the time I thrust those thoughts aside, too, for with them came always the realization that any hope I had of some day being his wife might soon be proven false.

Instead I dwelled on safer thoughts: my reunion with my father, my first meeting with my young stepmother, holding my infant brother in my arms, and how wonderful it would be to be at Langley again with Edward and our dogs and horses! The fear that my father would be angry with me had long passed. He would, I was sure, be as glad to see me as I would be to see him.

✳

I hoped, when we landed on England's shores, to hear that my father was either in London or some place nearby. To my great disappointment, no one could tell me exactly where he was; "somewhere in the north" was all I could learn, and, a little uncertain as to what I should do, I went directly and speedily to Westminster.

There, and this was most dismaying, I found the palace in a state of utter confusion. The royal apartments, including Maiden Hall, had caught fire on a very windy day the previous year and been burned out; much of the rest of the building had gone, too, but not, I am glad to say, my father's beautiful Painted Chamber. The fire fighters had saved most of the White Hall, and now, of course, extensive repairs and rebuilding were going on.

No one had remembered to tell me this particular bit of bad news, or I would certainly not have set foot in the dreary place. There were a few familiar faces in the depleted staff that was taking care of the almost deserted edifice, but nobody I cared about, and after an uncomfortable night there I almost wished myself back in The Hague.

The August sun was blazing hot, the grass on the banks of the Thames dry, and the smell of the filthy river enough to make anyone ill.

Had I wished to remain in the city I could have moved to York House, as they told me my father and his bride had done after the fire, or gone to the Tower. As I did not I stayed where I was, enduring the discomforts and noise of the workmen's hammers only long enough to allow my entourage the rest they needed before setting out again.

My father's exact whereabouts were still uncertain. In July, they told me, he and the army had laid seige to the castle of Caerlaverock, situated between Carlisle and Dumfries and so deep in bogs and swamps that it had taken them a week to capture it. He had then gone on to Kirkcudbright, but whether he was still there was in question.

The royal chamberlain, to whom I was talking, then suggested that I join the Queen at Cawood. "The Lady Margaret will know where the King is," he said. "She and her infant have been residing there at the Bishop's palace— the Bishop of York, I mean—for some weeks."

This advice seeming good, we decided to follow it and were soon on our way north. After the miserable years of what had almost been exile for me, it was indescribably wonderful to be riding through England's countryside again—and with nothing now to hurry us except the desire to be with my father. Even two days of rain did not lower my spirits, for it laid the dust, deepened the green of the grass, and gave the late summer flowers and the leaves of the trees a freshly washed appearance that delighted my eyes. The clearing skies brought men and women into the fields, waving and calling out to us as we passed, their faces so cheerful that all my people smiled and called back to them.

I remember Gretchen de Saux, trotting along beside me on a gentle gray palfrey, admitting that even her beloved Holland could not rival my England's beauty.

"Such variety!" she marveled. "Forests, rolling hills, sweet meadows, deep ravines! I had never realized how flat everything is at home."

"Just wait until we reach the moors," I told her. "The

heather should be in full bloom, stretching for miles—a soft, dull purple. You may not like the moors at first, but I suspect you will soon love them, as I do. Nothing but that purple on all sides under a blue sky! You can almost hear the bees humming with contentment."

Long before we arrived in Yorkshire *I* was humming with contentment, enjoying the hours in the saddle and every halt along the way. I remember most vividly a night we spent at Newark in a castle built by my great-grandfather, King John, a huge pile standing high on the bank of the River Trent, and another night at Selby, where we were entertained by the Benedictine monks in their quiet abbey.

I recall Newark because it is known as the gateway to the north and has always been one of our most important royal strongholds; Selby because it was there that we learned that Queen Margaret was no longer at Cawood.

We had halted at Selby merely to ask how to get there, for, although Cawood was not more than three miles distant, night was falling and we knew it was not on the road that continued on to York. The monk at the abbey gate indicated a small track that ran along on the left side of the Ouse, then inquired what was taking us there. When we told him, he shook his head.

"Her Grace set out two days ago for Rose Castle, the palace of the Bishop of Carlisle, where she joins King Edward. I'm afraid you will find no one at Cawood, my lady, and the road is narrow and rough. If you will remain with us instead, we will make you most heartily welcome."

This they did, and after a filling meal and a good night's sleep we rode off the next morning with Rose Castle as our new destination. I now saw no reason to speed after my stepmother; all we had to do was follow her party at our own pace, knowing that we would meet at my father's Court.

My steward, however, thought differently. He came to me, after paying for our nooning, with a worried countenance. "We are in trouble, my lady," he told me. "I find our money is almost gone. As you know, we had enough to take us to Cawood, but this further journey presents a serious problem. We must try to catch up with the Queen."

Gone was my plan to travel in a more leisurely manner and gone, as well, our pleasure in being on the road. Instead of enjoying the country around us, we watched for the cloud of dust ahead that could be the Lady Margaret's entourage, and, not seeing it, sought out places to spend our nights that would not further deplete our gold. Fountains Abbey—and beautiful it was—helped; then so did Middleham Castle, high on a windy hill overlooking moors and dales, where we were welcomed by old friends. But after that, what to do?

A night in an inn near Brough took our last coin of any value; then, after a day when we had only bread and cheese, we rode into Penryn. There I was able to sell a small shoulder brooch, which paid for our lodging and our breakfast, and we climbed into our saddles the next morning relieved to know that Rose Castle was now only an easy ride away.

It was also a pretty ride, for it was situated on a slight slope in the peaceful valley of the Caldew, a green oasis in the wooded countryside, so quiet and remote that it was hard to believe that busy Carlisle lay only six miles to the north.

I had, I think, expected to find it another huge stone pile like Middleham; instead, after we had made our way through the oak-filled park and clattered over the draw-bridge spanning a rather stagnant moat, we found our-selves in a sunny quadrangle surrounded by wooden bar-racks. There was no question but that my parent was in residence, for the courtyard was crowded with people in our royal livery, our standard fluttered on a rooftop, and I saw familiar faces as we approached the entrance. We reached it, I prepared to dismount, and there he stood, just inside the open doorway, still so tall and handsome, smiling at me.

With a squeal of joy I hurried out of the saddle and ran the rest of the way. A moment later I was where I had been longing to be: home in England, safe and in my lord father's warm embrace.

Twenty-One

For a moment all I could do was kiss my father and tell him how happy I was to be with him again. "But I thought to surprise you," I said, when he released me. "Instead I find you waiting for me."

He laughed. "My dear Elizabeth, I've known for several days that you were on your way here. Did you think you could travel through the countryside without some word of your progress reaching my ears? But now let me present you to our kind host, the Lord Bishop of Carlisle."

Just behind him stood a gaunt, redheaded man clad in the flowing robes of his office, watching me with a rather weary smile. I learned later that the continual uprisings of the Scots had, for years, made his life one of constant strife and peril, and that the task of defending the great border fortress of Carlisle was a burden few men would be willing or able to shoulder. And, as I look back, I realize that housing the household of the King of England could not have been a simple matter, either.

After his formal words of welcome he excused himself and I turned back to my father. "I am eager to meet the Lady Margaret," I told him dutifully. "My little brother Thomas, too, of course. Is he a healthy, thriving infant, Sire?"

My father's eyes lit up and he looked suddenly younger. "As you will see, Bette."

All this time my ladies had been hovering nearby, waiting to attend me to our apartments. I presented Lady de Saux to my father; then, while he greeted those he knew, I suggested to the chamberlain that he lead them there without me.

"Take me to my lady mother now," I said to my father, determined to overcome as soon as possible my natural reluctance to see someone taking my beloved mother's place.

"If you would like me to, certainly," was his instant reply. "We do not stand on ceremony here."

Turning, he strode toward the staircase with me close at his heels. Up we went, only a short flight; then we stood together and peered into a solar that was flooded, as it should be, with sunshine.

Two serving women were busy in one corner, three or four ladies chatted softly in another, plying their needles, and closer to the fire sat a young woman with an infant in her arms. Her robe was of some rich, heavy, silken stuff, and her hair—dark—was worn as I wear mine, braided and bound up in a crespine net. At first all I could see was her white linen barbette and gemmed circlet, for her face was hidden as she bent over the child. Then, as if aware of our scrutiny, she raised her head.

I had heard much of her loveliness, although, to be sure, it was her older sister Blanche who was famed for her beauty. But where, I asked myself, was it? An overlong nose, not unlike my mother's, a small chin, brown eyes—

Her gaze met my father's, she smiled, and she *was* beautiful. I could have warmed my hands at the affection that flowed between them, and that small feeling of resentment toward her that I was harboring in my heart melted completely away. I would have been a most selfish and unsympathetic daughter, I decided, to grudge my father this new source of happiness.

So without waiting for his words of presentation I ran to her chair and knelt before her, my arms outstretched.

"Dear lady," I said, "I am your daughter Bette!"

What she replied I do not know, but a moment later we were smiling into each other's eyes and I was crooning over the tiny bundle in her lap.

Rose Castle—even now the memory of it is like a sudden glimpse of the sun on a winter day. Never in my eighteen years had I been as simply housed, never had I been so fond of a temporary home. It was a small edifice, calling itself a castle, I suppose, because it was a bishop's residence, consisting altogether of a large hall, two solars, a chapel, kitchen, cellars, byre, and granary, all of wood. A stone peel tower, now partly finished, was being constructed in one corner of the quadrangle, but while we were there they stopped working on it and turned instead to the task of building stables for our draft horses.

My father paid for their labor, I am glad to say, and for the time other servants there spent fishing the royal pools at Tarnwadelin to give us a change of diet. But we could not pay for the inconvenience that Bishop Halton and his people suffered on our behalf, for, as Queen Margaret occupied one solar and my ladies and I the other, they moved themselves into that unfinished tower, where they must have been most uncomfortable.

Bishop Halton, I discovered, was very proud of his new quarters. "When our troubles with the Scots are over, I hope to replace all these wooden buildings with stone," he told us. "Ever since the town of Carlisle was gutted from wall to wall by fire eight years ago I have wanted to do so, but it has taken every penny I could scrape up to rebuild our cathedral there and to arm and provision our garrison."

I could understand his desire, but having lived almost entirely in huge, chill, drafty stone keeps with dozens of steep steps to climb, my ladies and I found the little solar a delightful change. We were, to be sure, extremely fortunate in the weather, as it was one of those rare warm autumns when one sunny day follows another, making it difficult to believe that winter, with its cold winds, pounding rains, sleet, and snow, is only a few weeks away.

My chief reason for liking Rose so much, however, was that we lived without ceremony or any formality. Our nobles and the army were stationed in Carlisle, and my father spent most of his time there with them; when he *was* with us we dined, supped, and passed our evenings together pleasantly and quietly, and when he was not they were even more quiet.

The one thought that disturbed this idyllic interval for me was the fear of what would happen when my year of mourning came to an end in November and, always part of that fear, the growing desire to see Humphrey—to discover whether the secret hope in my heart must now be forever forgotten.

While we were still at Rose there was no way of satisfying that desire, but one day I did broach the subject of my future to my father, thinking that his own marital happiness might make him more willing to leave mine in my hands.

I introduced the matter boldly, perhaps abruptly. "You promised me, in your last letter," I said, "that you would not arrange a second marriage for me until my year of mourning was over."

"So I did, Bette," was his reply. "And I have kept that promise, although I have been urged to change my mind by several extremely suitable noblemen both here and abroad."

"I have been hoping," I continued, "that you might promise me something else."

"What is that?"

"That, having done my duty by wedding Jan, you will allow me to choose my next husband myself—or remain single."

He looked at me, smiled, and shook his head. "I'm afraid I cannot make you such a promise, Bette, although I will not be unreasonable when that time comes. And before I do enter into any marriage contract for you I hope to secure your dowry; I do not mind paying your accounts, my dear child, but I would not want to give you away without the fortune to which you are entitled. Nor will I take any formal steps in betrothing you to anyone until we finally make peace with these rebellious Scots."

Someone entered then and I could not say anything more. His answer had reassured me to a certain extent, however, for it was obvious that he was not already working behind my back in this matter, and I retired from his presence almost content.

I had arrived at Rose on the seventeenth day of September. It was now October, and we still enjoyed good weather and our peaceful surroundings. Strolling, as I often did, around the castle grounds, I found it hard to believe that not more than six or seven miles distant our army was gathered, engaged in a campaign; a sporadic one, to be sure, but, still a campaign. We felt so secure here, probably because we knew that Carlisle with its high walls and great stone castle stood between us and any raiders from Scotland.

Early in my stay Bishop Halton himself took me to a spot that overlooked the countryside. He pointed first to the river on the southwest, then north.

"From the west bank of the Caldew down there," he told me, "to the south wall of Carlisle, everything belongs to me. The land and the one road that runs from here to the city gate, six miles away, all are contained in my bishop's franchise. No one can travel over it without my permission, nor can anyone cross Rose Bridge unless I allow it. Had this not been true, I would not have dared offer you and the Lady Margaret sanctuary here."

With our host's assurance adding to our feelings of

safety and pleasure in our tranquil existence, we drifted through the month. But as was to be expected, November brought an end to both the fair skies and our comfort.

The two solars, so delightfully warm when the sun poured into them for hours each day, were less inviting in bleak, windy weather; the outside staircases leading up to them became a hardship; and, with everyone forced to remain inside, even the larger Great Hall was miserably crowded.

It was particularly so one evening when my father brought a group of noblemen back from Carlisle to sup with us, something he had not often done during our stay at Rose. I found myself sitting beside John de Warenne, the elderly Earl of Surrey, and, to my great surprise, I saw Joanna's husband Rafe placed down the table on my father's left.

"I had no idea that my lord de Monthermer was in the north," I said to the Earl. "I thought he was at Marlborough with my sister."

My companion shook his grizzled head. "He is very much here, my lady, and has been for some time. I think you will be glad to learn that he is proving himself more than worthy of his new titles and honors. He fought very gallantly at Caerlaverock and has been so useful to us during this whole campaign that he is very high now in the King's favor."

"How happy Joanna must be!" I said. "I did not know my father had done more than recognize their marriage."

"He thinks of him as a son, I have heard him say, and woe to anyone who slights young Rafe in his presence."

"Well!" I marveled, smiling at him. "This news delights

me more than I can tell you, my lord. I played a part in their romantic story before going to Holland and, at the time, felt some of the force of my father's anger."

We said nothing further on the subject, but I remember sitting through the rest of the meal in what was almost amazement, finding my father's change of face wonderful but hard to believe. The moment we rose from the table I went to Rafe and greeted him affectionately.

He responded warmly; we had a good long talk about Joanna and the children, and, with a casualness I hoped was convincing, I slipped in a question or two about Humphrey.

He was here with the army, Rafe told me, and had assumed his late father's duties with grace and capability. Yes, he was well; no, he was not yet married but he might soon be.

For a moment I could not say a word; then I forced myself to smile and murmur something about this being good news.

"Who," I asked, trying desperately to sound natural, "is the fortunate lady?"

"That I do not know. I had a short and hurried conversation with the Countess his mother the last time I was in that part of the country, and she merely said that Humphrey had been talking to the father of a young noblewoman, hoping to gain his permission to wed her. Apparently she was not at liberty to reveal the name of the lady, and I did not, of course, press her. But as I cannot imagine anyone refusing such a great match for his daughter, I suspect we will hear of his betrothal one of these days."

Fortunately for me, someone joined us before I could respond and I was able to hide the searing pain until I reached my bedchamber and the privacy of my bed.

I cannot describe what I felt; all I can say is that I cared very little what happened to me in those empty years ahead.

When I rose the following morning and learned that we were all to move on to Carlisle the next day, I thought I could not do it. The prospect of meeting Humphrey was too painful, and I paced up and down my chamber, wondering how to avoid it.

Would my father allow me to take my household to Langley instead of Carlisle? As I had no money, I was powerless to make my own plans and in any case would need his permission to leave his Court. Then I remembered that all the arrangements had been concluded for the anniversary of Jan's death on November tenth, now only five days away. The ceremony would take place in Carlisle— to Carlisle I must go.

In the meantime, however, I could plead my mourning to remain in seclusion. Here at Rose Castle our life had been so informal that it had not been observed; at Carlisle it would be sufficient reason for me not to dine or sup in company.

Having come to this decision, I went about my preparations for our departure quietly, grateful for anything that kept me occupied. We were not expected at Carlisle Castle until late the next day, but when a feeble sun appeared early in the afternoon my ladies suggested that, as we were quite ready, we might take advantage of the better weather and ride there ahead of the others. Our small entourage could cover the six miles comfortably, leaving most of the servants and the baggage to follow us in the slower, cumbersome royal train.

I was more than willing; a brisk ride appealed to me, and we were soon in our saddles and on our way. The daylight was failing when we sighted the city which lies snugly within its walls, guarded on the east by Bishop Halton's River Caldew—we had followed it most of the time—and on the north by the River Eden; but we could still see our new home, the castle, free of the town, standing on a gently rising bluff at the northernmost end, towering at least sixty feet above the two rivers flowing past the walls.

As we waited for the guards to raise the portcullis, I said to Gretchen de Saux, who was still keenly interested in each new place she visited, "Most of Carlisle Castle was built more than a hundred years ago, but the palace where we will live is quite new and we should be extremely comfortable there. My father has made sure of that by glazing windows for us and seeing that all is in good repair. His people have been very busy the last few weeks!"

When we had crossed the triangular inner ward to the long range of buildings situated in the shadow of the north wall, we were met by the castle steward, or marshal as they called him up here, and taken to our quarters. I asked him to arrange for a light supper to be sent to us a little later, using this opportunity to explain to him that I would not be dining in the Great Hall until after November tenth, and why.

The moment he left us my spirits began to sag. I had time, now, to realize that Humphrey and I were probably under the same roof, and the heartache that I had held in abeyance all day took possession of me. I struggled, all through our supper, to seem as usual, but I must have been much quieter.

"You are tired, my lady," said Gretchen, shaking her head at me. "We will retire early."

Much as I wanted to be alone, I knew that this would be a mistake. The night held too many hours in which to lie awake, miserable and sleepless.

"I *am* tired," I replied, "but not sleepy. We might take a little stroll through the corridors—everyone will be in the dining hall for some hours yet—and then have a game or two of merels."

Several of my other ladies agreed that this was a good suggestion, and we ventured forth a few minutes later. As I had expected, the halls and stairs were empty except for the guards, and so was every chamber into which we peered. We had climbed the stairs again and were on our way back when the sound of music reached us; and one of the ladies, darting off to an open door, turned and beckoned to us.

"Come," she said. "There's a gallery here. You can look down into the hall."

Fool that I was, I followed the others and took my place at the railing. The tables had been cleared away and the company was dancing, a pretty and lively tableau. Realizing almost immediately that we could be seen, too, I stepped back behind Gretchen and into a shadowed corner where I would not be so visible. I could still see a few of the dancers, however, and during one of the slower measures I found myself looking across the hall at one particular couple who seemed to be enjoying themselves more than the others.

The man was Humphrey, and a lady so beautiful that I

felt ill with jealousy. She had great dark eyes that were laughing up into his, white, white skin, a slender body, and, as she made a graceful step, I glimpsed a dainty foot much smaller than mine.

Who was she? I had no idea. From their behavior I was certain that this must be the high-ranking lady he planned to marry. I should, I knew, leave the gallery immediately and stop torturing myself; instead, I watched every move they made, every smile, every glance, every touch, until at last the music ended and they walked off the floor.

Only then did I lead my ladies back to our apartments. To my surprise I did sleep that night—perhaps because I now knew the worst.

I did very little the following day, remaining mostly in my privy chamber. When the Lady Margaret and my father arrived toward nightfall I visited them and my infant brother and told them my decision to stay more or less in seclusion until my year of mourning was over.

"It is only four more days," I added hurriedly, "and then I thought I might, with your permission, Sire, join Edward at Langley."

My father looked at me in silence for a moment; then he nodded, his face telling me nothing. "If that is what you want, Bette," he replied. "Suppose we wait and see what the weather is? And who knows, you might change your mind. We would rather keep you with us, of course."

Not wishing to prolong the conversation I excused myself and, as I neared the door, saw him reach for his young son Thomas. The laugh I loved to hear and had missed in recent years rang out just after I crossed the threshold, and I returned to my rooms with it echoing in my ears.

How happy he was with his new family, and how miserable I was! His life so full—mine so empty! A flood of bitterness swept over me as I remembered all the lessons I had been taught: a King's daughter cannot expect to wed for love. Royal marriages are arranged to promote peace and trade with our neighbors.

Neither can a King marry whom he pleases. That, too, I knew. But my father had found love in both his unions, love and the children I still hungered for.

Twenty-Two

The days passed slowly, broken only by short walks during the warmest hours on part of the south wall. We were taken there, soon after our arrival at the castle, by the marshal. "Our ladies have always walked here," he told us. "And once, back in 1296, an unusually stalwart group of them drove off a band of invading Scots by pelting them with stones and other missiles from this very spot. The enemy had set the city on fire and our men were off fighting the blaze, leaving no one here but the ladies to defend the castle—which they most certainly did!"

It was a stirring tale, and it gave us something new to talk about. I welcomed any fresh topic at this particular time, anything, in fact, that would take my mind off my own troubles.

My ladies, during those walks, moved from side to side
of the wall, drawn by the crowds of armed men riding in
and out of the courtyard, our constant reminder that we,
too, were involved in warfare with the Scots, however
sporadic it might be. I, not wanting the hurt of seeing
Humphrey, even from a distance, kept my feet on the far
side of the ramparts and my eyes away from the cobbles.

It was an effort, but everything was an effort. I had no
appetite, I found it difficult to play games, and music made
me strangely restless. My only source of comfort was the
thought that this state of affairs would not last much
longer and, having been schooled at an early age to hide
my emotions, I forced myself to seem much as usual.

Not even unhappiness can stop time from passing, and
I awakened on the morning of November tenth with a
definite feeling of relief. Today I must devote entirely to
mourning the memory of Jan, but tomorrow I would be
free to resume my old way of life, and soon, I hoped, be
on my way to Langley.

So, with the Lady Margaret on one side, Lady Gretchen
on the other, and the rest of my household close behind us,
I rode from Carlisle Castle to the church of the friar
preachers—the Dominicans—where we had arranged for
masses to be performed for my poor young husband's
soul.

My thoughts on the short journey were all his, and I
tried to remember only the sunny hours we had spent
together. The most pleasant of these I described to my
companions as we clattered over the rough cobbles, but
mostly I was silent and so were they.

From the moment we entered the church I had no
further need to discipline either my thoughts or my ac-

tions. The solemn ceremony held me in thrall—the black-robed monks, the sonorous chanting voices, the drifting incense, the flickering candles all elevated and comforted me, then left me, at last, feeling calm and cleansed.

The wonderful peaceful mood remained with me during the lavish dinner I provided for the friar preachers. Then, as was proper, I spent what was left of the day in prayer, retiring early to my bed.

I rose refreshed, determined to see my father at the first possible moment to ask when I might set out for Langley; but before I sent for our chamberlain he came to me.

"The King will be with us for supper," he told me, "and he wishes you to join him and the Lady Margaret at the high table. You will be seated beside him tonight, and he hopes you will take part in and enjoy the evening's entertainment."

My heart sank. Undoubtedly Humphrey would be there, and his unbearably beautiful betrothed. "I would like a private audience with his Grace," I said to the chamberlain. "Immediately, if you can arrange it for me."

He shook his head. "I'm sorry, my lady," he replied regretfully. "The King has already gone to the army encampment and will not return to the castle until suppertime."

After he left me I tried to think of some way of avoiding my father's invitation. It was really a command, I knew, and although I could plead illness, perhaps, it would now have to be a sudden indisposition. It was apparent that he had prepared a special evening to mark the end of my year of mourning, and if I failed to appear it would displease him.

I was still turning the matter over in my mind when my ladies suggested a walk on the walls, and I climbed the stairs almost hoping to twist my ankle on one of the worn stones. After we had taken a turn or two up and down the ramparts, something in the courtyard below caught my ladies' attention. While they peered over, talking and laughing among themselves, I wandered off, glad to have a moment alone.

I think I was staring down at the river Caldew, wishing I could follow it back to peaceful Rose Castle, when I heard footsteps behind me. Swinging around, I found myself face to face with Humphrey. He was out of breath and before he could speak I gave him a little nod and greeted him formally.

"It is good to see you looking so well, my lord Earl," I said stiffly. "I was sorry to hear of your father's death, but I must congratulate you on the honors that have come your way and, of course, on your future happiness."

He looked at me in what seemed to be surprise. Perhaps he had expected me to be more friendly—God knows what he expected! *I* certainly did not, but I realized that if I was not to break down I must maintain a distant attitude. My legs were shaking under me and I had to blink rapidly to keep back the tears, but I controlled myself enough to give him a polite smile.

"Much has happened since we last saw each other, has it not?" I went on hurriedly. "But how fortunate we both are. Here I am, home at last and eager to resume my old life free of any entanglements, and you, my lord, about to assume fresh and delightful ties."

"Bette—" he said slowly, frowning as he stared at me. "What do you mean? What are you trying to say to me? I

asked where you were, then I ran up those steps thinking
—and now—" He hesitated, braced his shoulders, then
continued, still staring at me. "It is certainly true that I
hope to assume new ties; I have been hoping to for a long
time, and I came here to you at the first possible moment
to tell you—"

"It was good of you to do so," I interrupted, clinging
to the last of my composure. "As an old friend, I want
to hear all about it. But you will finish your story another
time, perhaps? Here come my ladies, and I am too cold to
stand here another minute."

My ladies *were* approaching, to my great relief, and I
held out my hand to Humphrey in an unmistakable
gesture of dismissal. He bent over it, moved away, then
turned and almost ran to the stairs.

Pulling up my cloak to hide my face, I called to my
ladies, "I'm cold! Come." A moment later I was descending the winding stairs, hearing Humphrey's footsteps ahead
of me down the dark well.

By the time we reached my privy chamber I was trembling all over and my teeth were chattering. Lady Gretchen, noticing this when I spoke to the tiring woman who
helped me out of my cloak, ran to my side.

"You have a chill, my lady!" she exclaimed, her face
concerned. "I'll send for some hot wine. Lie down and
cover yourself with that fur bedcover."

I demurred, but they all buzzed around me like bees;
and, to tell the truth, I was grateful for the warming drink
and the excuse to rest quietly for a while. My encounter
with Humphrey had unnerved me completely, and I was
still so shaken that I felt I could not bear up another
minute.

After I emptied the goblet of steaming wine I pulled the fur coverlet up to my chin and drifted off to sleep. It was dark when I awakened, and Lady Gretchen, nearing me stir, rose from a seat by the fire and came to my bedside.

"How do you feel, my lady?" she asked me. "Shall I send word to the King that you are not well enough to join him for supper?"

Earlier that day I had tried to think how best to avoid going to the dining hall; now that I could easily do so I realized that this would be a mistake. I had taken these first difficult steps to show Humphrey that he had not broken my heart and I must take a few more tonight. After that I should be able to meet him, as I inevitably would, without too much pain.

Fortunately my long sleep had left me rested and more at ease, and feeling that I could face this second ordeal reasonably well, I told Lady Gretchen so and asked her to summon my tiring woman. Needless to say I chose my loveliest robe and made sure that my hair was dressed in its most becoming fashion. Knowing that I looked my best would help—and I needed help!

I think I must have been reasonably successful, for when I took my seat beside my father he gave me an approving smile.

"I am happy to have my beautiful daughter with me tonight," he said warmly. "Happy and proud. Enjoy yourself, my dearest child! You have certainly earned all the pleasure I shall now try to give you."

While I was thanking him, our usher brought Humphrey to the dais and seated him on my other side. I had not expected this, although I suppose I should have; he was, after all, the highest-ranking young nobleman present and I was the guest of honor. I turned and greeted him, thanking God that this was not our first meeting since I learned of his imminent betrothal.

As it was, I was able to smile calmly and make some commonplace remark about the evening's entertainment. Before he could reply, my father leaned over me and asked him a question about the latest Scottish raid.

To my great relief they continued their discussion through most of the meal, and the servants were clearing away the other tables before my father turned back to the Lady Margaret, sitting on his left. I heard him apologizing for his rudeness; then, taking my courage in both hands, I spoke again to Humphrey.

"Forgive me for leaving you so abruptly this afternoon," I said. "I was suddenly terribly cold. But now you must tell me what you were going to tell me then, and what I have been wanting to know—the name of the beautiful lady."

"The beautiful lady?"

"The lady you were going to tell me about." The musicians, in the gallery over our heads, chose that moment to begin playing, drowning out the rest of my reply; and as I was about to repeat it, the Master of the Dance appeared before us.

"You will lead the dancing this evening, your ladyship," he announced. "With the Earl of Hereford, if you please."

As Humphrey helped me down from the dais he spoke softly but urgently into my ear.

"For the love of God, Bette, explain what you are talking about! *What* lady?"

"The lady you plan to marry. With the dark eyes and hair. Rafe told me—"

"Rafe told you I was going to marry someone with dark hair and eyes?"

"No, no! He said that your mother told him you had asked some nobleman for his daughter's hand. I saw you dancing with her here."

We had been walking slowly onto the floor, whispering hurriedly to each other. Now Humphrey gave a short laugh, and I glanced up to find him looking at me, his eyes sparkling with amusement. "What a ridiculous business!" he said. "So that was what you meant today—why you behaved like an icicle!"

By this time we had taken our place and the other couples were joining us. Then, as the first note was struck, Humphrey spoke again.

"The lady I *hope* to marry has golden hair and blue eyes. The nobleman is the King of England, and I have asked him for his daughter not only once but several times —every time I've had a chance, in fact, since I heard her husband was dead!"

I stood, staring at him, deaf to everything but the unbelievable, wonderful words I had heard him say.

"Dance!" he hissed in my ear. "Dance, Bette! Dance!"

With a start, I realized that the musicians were already playing the first measure and everyone was waiting for me to begin. As swiftly as I could I fitted my steps to the notes and, a bit awkwardly as always, Humphrey followed my example.

I was still so bemused that it was a minute or two before I was aware that we were performing the Danse au Chapelet. Fortunately my feet had known it, for I was moving through the familiar figures without a mistake.

Toward the end of the dance I was able to speak to him again, to ask him the two questions I must have answered. "What did my father say, Humphrey? And why didn't you come to me when I arrived in Carlisle?"

"He has not yet given me an answer, and the last time I asked him for one he commanded me not to approach you until your year of mourning was ended."

"But then tonight—?" We were separated before I could say anything more, and I was now more bewildered than ever. If my father meant me to wed someone else, why had he not told Humphrey so? I glanced over to where he was sitting and saw that he was watching me, his face so impassive that I felt chilled. Chilled and angry. Humphrey must have told him that *I* wanted to wed *him*.

Why had he not agreed to our union? And if he was determined to keep us apart, why had he allowed the marshal and Master of the Dance to pair us this evening?

I could not believe that my father would play cat and mouse with us. Perhaps he had not known that Humphrey and I were to be thrown together tonight; perhaps there was some reason why he must arrange another foreign alliance for me.

As all these thoughts raced through my mind, the moment arrived for Humphrey to kiss me. His lips touched mine, and, suddenly not caring who saw us or where we were, I kissed him with all the love I had been holding in my heart. He responded instantly, his kiss the deepest and most passionate I had ever known.

When I raised my head I looked again at my father. Let him be angry, let him—

He was smiling. He was smiling directly at me, and, as I caught my breath, hardly daring to think what this could mean, he gave a little nod, first at me and then at Humphrey, threw back his head, and began to laugh!